By the same author

*

THE LAST GRIFFIN
DRAGONS AND MORE

LINK OF THREE

"Your war has drawn us very close," s[...]
stranger when he meets Ann, Pete[...]
Jessica on the beach. Escaping fro[...]
bombs of 1940 to "a safe place", the[...]
a more mysterious hazard awaits them[...]
is this demanding stranger? Why do[...]
never survive in the village of Pengaron?[...]
menacing forces belong to the rocky c[...]

Link
of
Three

MILDRED DAVIDSON

CHATTO & WINDUS

London

Published by
Chatto & Windus Ltd
40 William IV Street
London WC2N 4DF

*

Clarke, Irwin & Co Ltd
Toronto

*British Library Cataloguing
in Publication Data*

Davidson, Mildred
    Link of three.
    I. Title
    823'. 9'1J   PZ7.D/
    ISBN 0-7011-2486-5

Printed and bound in Great Britain by
Redwood Burn Ltd
Trowbridge and Esher.

It was always a nuisance, being saddled with girls, Peter thought.

His father had said: "Take your cousin if you're visiting the fair. She needs looking after now she's no dad. No mother either while your Aunt Lucy's out at work all day."

Well, Ann with her tortoise-shell spectacles was a skinny little owl, and Peter had got used to dragging her with him, especially since the war started. But to have her friend Jessica come too was straining his good nature.

Jessica lacked nothing as far as Peter could see. She had a father who was in the Civil Service and a mother who wore fox furs. She had a dog, two cats, a tortoise, a large garden, nice clothes that mustn't get spoiled, and two older brothers who sported sleek hair styles and naval uniforms. Except that she was in the same form as Ann at school Peter couldn't see what they had in common.

Ann came suddenly close.

"Look," she said.

On her unclasped palm there lay a tiny silver threepence, worn and rare. It was a last-minute present from her uncle.

"I shan't spend it," she said, tying it into her handkerchief.

"C'mon," said Peter. "I want to have a go at the rifles."

Noise and smells had been rising all morning on the common and were in full spate by dinner-time. The fair was doing its best during daylight hours to make people forget that armies were marching just on the other side of the Channel. Only the constant military uniforms brought their reminder: khaki, navy, airforce blue, and black. With the spring the trees had revolted and raised arms sleeved in blossom. White, pink, glowing rose.

The children wandered between cracking rifles and mechanical laughter. Everything had the attraction of ugliness. Plaster clowns with gaping red mouths rolled their heads. Balls flew, plates dropped, baby-doll prizes swung just out of reach. The girls shied at the noise: croupish and horridly exploding.

Peter jangled the coins in his pocket. A rifle hot from many palms was swivelled towards him. He took up his stand the way he'd seen the uniformed young men do. The stall-holder gave him advice and Peter's shots popped.

"Too far out," said the man. "Have another go."

Peter had another go.

"Too bad, feller. Try again later."

Peter turned and jutted his chin at the girls.

"Good shot," he said. And Ann nodded loyally.

"Let's get away from here," muttered Jessica.

A flow of music came from across the stalls, sliding along soldiers' broad backs, refusing to be stamped out by heavy boots. It poured over Ann like great refreshing waters in the heat of the day. The merry-go-round, of course.

She forgot about the others as it drew her on to where glossy black manes flowed wildly and fixedly from white, red, orange, and yellow steeds. Her father had held her on one when she was very small. That same tall gallant father had been killed in Belgium very early in the war.

"I want to go on the horses," Ann told herself with quiet determination.

"Wait for me."

It was Jessica from a distance, hating to be on her own. Peter must have gone back to the ranges.

Together they clambered into the circle. A brawny arm would have swept the small girl with glasses onto an inside mount, but Ann escaped to the edge and found herself a large white steed with jetty eyes.

"Hold on," came a man's voice as the horses began to crest and sink.

Peter flung into view at the last minute.

"Kid's stuff," he yelled against the music, cupping his mouth. "Watch the manure."

"Blinkers," retorted Jessica, joyously slapping her horse's hard glazed rump.

"I gotta 'orse!" Peter yelled as they came round for the second time.

After that they could just see his mouth open.

Ann closed her eyes and felt herself soar dizzily. The feet of her Pegasus were splayed, she knew, in a glorious scattering motion. Gradually the spikes of the day grew blunted in her memory: her mother exhausted from work at the hospital; a struggle into a tight dress that had to last another year at least; and always the ingrained sadness of the little house, with a photograph of her father staring its reminder.

"Too pale. Doesn't get out enough," her uncle had said of her that morning. "Should have a spell in the country."

But what did it matter when the wind was soft on her cheek, and she and her cobble-eyed steed were close to great triumphs? The movement was intoxicating. Worlds rushed by and came again but always the horse swung her round and away, for both were bound in the circle's keeping for ever and for ever. . .

Mechanical laugher spilled and rattled at a distance. The music of the hurdy-gurdy was slowing. As Ann opened her eyes in some disappointment the fair itself whirled like a multi-coloured top.

For a while the three children joined forces and wandered stoically between frying onions and candy floss. Around them people were fantastically merry as if sensing that Britain's hour of danger was near. It was quieter at the far end of the fair where a brown booth stood encircled by billboards.

"Look," said Jessica, blazing into life. "There's a fortune-teller."

"C'mon," said Peter. "She doesn't want us."

7

"How d'you know?"

"Cost you half-a-crown."

"How d'you *know*?"

"Mother said. One came to the doorstep and told her fortune. Wasn't worth it, she said."

Jessica — tired, defiant, sick of rifle ranges — flushed pink like a heating shell fish.

"What d'you want to know your future for?" goaded Peter. "I can tell you what's going to happen. Wait till the Jerries start dropping their bombs here. You'll be evacuated, that's what."

The suddenness with which Jessica went from pink to white startled even Peter. She looked as though she would drop.

"No I won't," she said, her lips scarcely moving. "Mummy wouldn't let me."

Peter gulped air like a fish. Ann, with quick perception, intervened.

"You have a go," she said to Jessica. "Take the three-pence. It's silver after all."

She undid her handkerchief and stared, a little reluctantly, at the tiny coin.

Peter snorted.

"What d'you want to give her that for? You know she's got more money than you."

"It's special somehow," said Ann.

Jessica had an unexpected pang of guilt.

"No, I can't take it. *You* have a try."

Peter snorted again.

"I'm off."

"I'll wait for you, Ann," said Jessica mulishly.

"Oh, but I didn't mean —"

Ann found herself, still dazed from the merry-go-round, being propelled towards the booth. The place was quiet at the moment for the gypsy had closed down to have her lunch. Gaudy lettering started from a billboard: *This lady has second sight.*

"I've got second sight too," said Ann, clutching wildly at her glasses.

"Ha, ha," said Peter heavily.

He obviously hadn't moved far.

"It's all right," called a voice from the interior of the booth. "I'm ready now."

With shock Ann found herself close to the curtain that was drawn across to leave a mere peephole. Jessica gave a last push and Ann was through.

"Take the stool," said the woman and with one tug at the drapes she separated Ann entirely from the outside world.

The place, which was just big enough for the two of them to sit together, was dimly lit by an oil lamp. It was quiet too, padded with velvet. As Ann's eyes adjusted to the gloom her attention was riveted by the gypsy's face. The woman was as dark and brooding as she ought to be, but she was young also, with a touch of glamour about her scarlet lips and hooped earrings. Yet the eyes were as old and as hard as centuries-formed granite.

"Suppose it *is* half-a-crown," thought Ann, suddenly afraid.

The gypsy studied her face for a minute. Then she said: "You have silver with you?"

Ann could do nothing but hold out her palm with the tiny threepence at its centre. It looked a poor enough thing as the gypsy fixed her gaze on it. Then her own dark palm came down on top and rested there.

Everything in the booth began to blur; Ann's glasses tingled, dislodged.

"Hold on," came the gypsy's voice as if from a distance. Ann closed her eyes, still feeling giddy. Now she could let herself flow back into the rhythm of the merry-go-round, rising and circling. . . .

The gypsy raised her hand from the girl's, and Ann knew she had to return. As she opened her eyes she could see only the silver threepence, a pin-prick of light

9

in the distance. Yet it was beginning to grow, and spinning as it came towards her. Ann gasped as the light scintillated in the darkened surroundings. It was like a flat disc of moonlight, beautiful, she told herself, much more beautiful than the worn-out coin. If only she could enter its movement — like riding the merry-go-round —

Gradually, as if her desire had some power in this place, the circle was slowing. When the disc appeared to have reached its full size it rolled with a dignity as of the moon's mass. Ann could begin to see a pattern emerging around the edges, a pattern that included four figures placed like the corners of a square, with wild hair and bright eyes and disturbingly familiar —

Everything was shrinking before she could take in the significance of those faces; the disc was spinning away into the distance, winding back into a mere fraction of metal. The light went from it as the music had died from the merry-go-round, until only the coin winked from the middle of her palm.

"Oh," gasped Ann again as the still outer world of the booth and the gypsy and the suffocating velvet surged back.

"Go," said the woman, tugging open the curtain and letting a wider world of daylight assail the girl. "It has nothing more to tell you."

"Ann," exclaimed Jessica as her friend stumbled out, "you're white as a sheet. Whatever did she say to you?"

"Nothing," said Ann blinking in the sunshine.

Suddenly she turned, remembering that she still held the coin. Loth as she was to let it go, honesty made her extend her palm towards the open curtain. The gypsy's answer was to rear up in the entrance to her booth, forcing all three children to look at her.

"I see three linked in one here," she said. "You must hold to that link now it is made. It will protect on the path that is waiting."

She passed a hand in front of her eyes and her voice grew harsh.

10

"Hold hard to it, I say. There is one I see breaking and bringing danger — "

Ann felt her arm seized.

"C'mon," said Peter.

The woman turned away into her booth.

"Oh," said Ann when they'd gone further. "She didn't take the threepence."

"I should think not," said Peter. "Not for that tripe."

"We're going to stay together, though," said Jessica, "aren't we? She warned us — "

"Humph!" said Peter.

He supposed he'd promised his father after all.

"Stick by your cousin Ann," said Peter's father. "She'll need you more when you're evacuated."

Peter gripped his bottom lip between his teeth. The war did things to you in a strange way. There was a time when he wouldn't be seen with girls. Not in front of Spiffins and Mark and the rest of the gang. Now the whole Boys' Grammar School was being evacuated and relatives, young and old, were being shuttled along too. The bombs had made a difference all right.

"It's good that your schooling will go on and in a nice place like Wales," said his father. "It's a worry the less for us, you know."

Peter didn't answer. Part of him wanted to stay.

"And that you'll have a bit of the family with you."

Peter still said nothing, only nodding by way of

11

compromise. His father gazed out over the vegetable allotment he had painstakingly cultivated for the past few months.

"They say it's a good year for orchids. Weather's right I suppose."

"Yes," said Peter at last. And his father knew he could rely on him.

The bombing meant that summer holidays were virtually cancelled. It was after a night of fires and sirens that Peter's school met. Luggaged and parcelled they marched in crocodile formation to the station, past stretchers piled at the roadside.

Old Turtle, the history master, led Peter's class straight to the vaulted platform, between dense throngs of khaki-bulked troops and parents waiting to see them off. Jessica had joined Ann at the last minute, choosing when necessity compelled to go with her friend. Near the train stood her tall smart mother defying the war in a perky new hat with a rose on its forward brim.

"Darling," said the woman, with all the haste of departure on them, "you'll take care and write and let me know what to send on. And stick with Ann, won't you. And no more nightmares, remember. You're getting away from the bombs and you won't be alone. Just write often and let me know where you are and if you need anything. I'll come and see you whenever I can — soon, I promise."

As the Great Western pulled out old Turtle streamed conversationally on as if he were in his classroom.

"The route we are taking follows the division between the old kingdoms of Mercia and Wessex. The Mercians were a business-like people but in Wessex there was more magic. . ."

The train chugged through bomb-shattered areas where fires were still burning and cratered buildings rose out of rubble. Then it gathered speed and ran out into a hedged and ditched countryside.

As the children pressed faces to the windows they

12

could see no indication of where they were he

"Of course not," said Peter knowledgeably. "I
Jerries invade us and we've taken down all the plac
names, they won't know where they are, will they?"

A stiff breeze which had blown since early morning was
making blankets of steam as the train veered in direction.
Gradually the fresh excitement of morning passed into a
leaden afternoon, and everything grew strange. Trees were
dwarfed against hills and smoky-green valleys sprouted
shrub-like against a wall of barren mountain.

Through a concourse of coal trucks they steamed into a
sizeable town. The train stopped with angry snorts like a
tired horse, and they all tumbled out, creased to the bone.
A Welsh voice drew them into the station and another one
proclaimed:

"Welcome to Abertowyn. You boys will be billeted as
close to one another as possible. And as close to the school
you are to go to as we can make it."

"Please sir," said Peter when his name was called, "there
are three of us."

The man looked up.

"Not a brother of these two, are you?"

"No, but I promised — "

"We'll have to split you up. Nothing else to be done,
boy."

"We're together," said Peter quickly.

The man frowned. Demanding personal attention, were
they? He'd hold this lot over to the end.

When that came in sight it was nearly tea-time and the
billeting officers were plainly anxious to get the children
away to their new homes. Only the difficult ones remained.

"Not a place to put you girls together now," said the
man. "Not one family are you?"

Jessica showed alarm.

"Hardly anything left on the books, you see. . ."

Peter stood his ground. "It's important," he said, "that
we're not separated."

13

Ann groped into her handkerchief. Her
...tered a tiny metal edge. They *would* stay
...as certain.

...man with the billeting party nosed her way
...e.

...try their luck with me. I am going up to
...

...week's party from Swansea boarded around
Duffryn?" asked the man. "It must be swollen like a squid
already with that lot."

"You needn't tell me," said the woman with an eager
bossiness about her. "It's not my own village I am thinking
of. There's Pengaron, over to the coast. A nice quiet place
and not had an evacuee yet."

The man gave a half whistle.

"Not a place I'd think of for children, that, Miss Jones.
Old wives' tales, you know."

The woman snapped her fingers for answer.

"You three keep with me," she ordered. "We are
catching the next train up."

There was another journey, this time through a valley,
the sky all the time signalling storm. Forty minutes of
swaying weariness landed them in Duffryn. They could
see the village lying to the right of the railway, a neat
conglomeration of buildings with hills rising behind. To
the left the open country was given over to farmsteads.

"Three chapels, five pubs," said Miss Jones. "You see
we're alive in these parts. There's a bit of a school too.
Nice for you girls, though Peter will have to travel each
day to Aber. Pengaron's a bus ride from here. It's nearer
the sea, too."

With this comfort she lodged her charges against the
station wall.

"Hardly a bus now," she said. "Wait for me just ten
minutes. I'm going up the farm. See if there's a van can
take us."

She collected a bicycle and pedalled off. It was nearer

14

a quarter of an hour before Miss Jones swept back with a young man driving a farm vehicle.

"This them?" he said cheerily. "Sure you can't go other places?"

"Quite," said Miss Jones firmly. "Why the fuss?"

"Pengaron's all right by me if that's what they want. Jump in, you lot. A fine evening this for you to be coming to Wales."

They heaved themselves and their luggage into the back.

"Now for the fastnesses," said Miss Jones.

"That means strongholds," thought Peter. But to the other two it sounded as if food was still a long way off. Ann clutched her gas-mask box into the pit of her stomach.

They drove north and west from Duffryn into thick country, heading straight for a sky that was sickly green. Miss Jones pointed to where she lived. A gate, a rutted track, hedge and rising ground was all they could glimpse of her parents' farm. Jessica was beginning to think she had never seen such a stretch of country containing so few inhabitants. Theirs might be the only vehicle on the road.

Pengaron, when they reached it, was marked by a handful of stone cottages and a lane that led to a centre — a low chapel, a post office, a couple of stores. Jessica didn't believe they had actually arrived.

Miss Jones hitched herself out of the van and with a skip and a run disappeared into the post office. A few minutes later she repeated the process in reverse, flushing the van with cold air.

"The Pinchers it is," she said. "Not a Welsh name that. Back a bit. First cottage as we turned."

This time Miss Jones took the three children and their luggage right in with her. Mrs. Pincher was a lean woman, more apron than body. She sat so awfully upright that Peter wondered that she did not sway before Miss Jones's spirited onslaught. With iron in her spine she looked dubiously at the three children. In fact she was more struck by what she saw than by anything Miss Jones could say.

"We've a bed spare," she said slowly. "Big enough. There's sheets in the drawers. But only the girls — "

"Isn't there a naval man next door?" Miss Jones struck in. "At the post office they said. Perhaps for Peter — "

"Captain Marks is a retired gentleman who lost his wife in the spring. There'd be no woman to look after the boy. He'd be needing someone."

"With a motherly neighbour, though — ?"

The two stared into each other's eyes. Had Miss Jones not been preoccupied with the vanishing daylight she might have noticed the effect of her last words on Mrs. Pincher. At last the woman said:

"The Captain's got his old fishing boat, you see. Goes out a lot. The boy would have to fend for himself."

"Beautiful," said Miss Jones rising like fresh bread. "Divide it whichever way you like. There's my tea standing cold in Duffryn. But worth the good cause. You'll see me again when the sky's looking better."

A few words in Welsh and Miss Jones was out on the doorstep and flitting back into the van before Mrs. Pincher could express her outrage.

"Well!" she exclaimed when the motor started. "There's a fine one, abandoning you easy like that. Well!"

The children made no move.

"Up the stairs with you girls," said Mrs. Pincher. "I had better not think what my husband will say."

Peter carried his luggage to the next doorstep and waited. It was a little while before a man's figure began to loom out of the storm. In the bewitched light there was something distinctly and powerfully wild about him.

"What's this?" demanded the Captain throatily.

Mrs. Pincher appeared on hearing the man's voice. With Welsh speed she repeated Miss Jones's arguments for taking in castaways.

"Nasty thing this war. We can all do a bit to help."

"My wars have never included children," growled the Captain in tones that were distinctly not Welsh. " 'Ceptin'

16

cabin boys, and they were at th'other end."

Mrs. Pincher went off suddenly to rescue her boiling kettle and the man, puffing and blowing, let himself into the cottage. Peter remained undecided on the doorstep.

"Stem that draught," barked the Captain.

Peter hitched his luggage through the door.

"Well," said the Captain, looking down from a very great height, "so I've actually got a boy in my keeping, have I? Fee, Fi, Fo, Fum, and all that."

He showed Peter one or two things around the cottage, adding by way of making him feel at home: "There are rules about any place. But especially about this one."

He stalked out with customary suddenness and Peter was left solitary. The heavy ticking of an oak-cased clock penetrated the stillness. The boy felt hungry: it had been short rations all day and those had been only paste sandwiches. He thought someone should order him to wash after his day's travelling and invite him to a meal. The Captain, however, had said: "There's the kitchen. There's a room for ye. There are rules everywhere in the house, you'll find."

Peter wondered if one of the rules was that you made your own meals or alternatively that you didn't eat at all. He thought about calling next door to see if Ann and Jessica were faring better, but Mrs. Pincher had not invited him to go back and he hesitated to intrude. His father had said: "Don't make a nuisance of yourself."

He sat dolefully on a pallet bed which was covered with an old dusty counterpane. He looked out of the window. He counted the seconds along with the clock whose ticking in the silence reached to the rooms upstairs. Rain was beginning to drive at the window-panes. The heat from the day's travel, with its lugging of suitcases and its stops and its starts, had gone cold on the boy. He shivered inside and out with the first overriding feeling of homesickness he had ever known.

There came the click and the precise slamming of a

door. The wind was strong enough to propel even the Captain forward as he entered the house in a hurry. Peter, forgetting his awe of the man, moved speedily towards the sound.

He looked from the top of the narrow stairs as his benefactor, spouting with wind and rain, filled the small hall. He had in his hand a newspaper-wrapped parcel, the scent from which the boy could not have mistaken in a million years. As Peter appeared on the staircase the Captain looked up, then he waved his parcel in the air, sending round the whole house the rich smell of kipper.

"Come on, boy," he said. "We'll have some tack at least. Hope you're used to ship's biscuit."

Ann and Jessica found themselves in a raftered room. The wood had its own strong scent and no doubt provided a home for spiders and beetles of multiple race and colour.

"You will have to tread careful," said Mrs. Pincher about the lumber that was stored there. "We are not using this."

"The Pinchers don't want us," announced Jessica when she and Ann had come up for the night.

Ann thought Mrs. Pincher kind in her own way. She'd asked them about their homes and listened to their stories about the bombing. She had given them a meal before her husband got home but had refused to eat herself. Mr. Pincher was a hedger and ditcher, she said, and sometimes worked on farms at a distance.

This evening when he got in after a long walk through the storm she gave all her attention to his gruff tiredness. She suggested that the girls go to bed early so that a candle would not be necessary in their room.

"I will leave you this chest-of-drawers to put your belongings in," she told them. "You've no need to go in the wardrobe. There's things best not disturbed."

Now as they were left alone in the dusky half-light Jessica examined the furniture with intense suspicion.

"I don't like wardrobes," she said. "Mummy says they look like coffins. I always look into mine at home before I go to bed. In case. . ."

She tried the handle and found it wouldn't open. The key, however, was in the lock.

"Don't," said Ann. "She asked us not to. She'll think she can't trust us."

"Nonsense," said Jessica. "I'll never sleep if I don't look inside."

The key clicked loudly. Mr. and Mrs. Pincher sitting quietly together in the cottage living-room might well have heard.

"Oh Jessica," said Ann.

The belongings of the cupboard would have spilled out had they not been so closely packed. Instead they bulged forcefully forward: a mighty pre-war collection of Mrs. Pincher's best linen in addition to ancient garments.

"She won't know we've been in," said Jessica, shame-faced.

She pushed against the door.

"Oh," she panted. "Something's stuck."

Ann went round the bed to help. Even their combined weight couldn't force the lock to catch.

"We'll have to leave it," said Ann reluctantly.

"She's bound to notice."

"I suppose so."

"Stupid!" said Jessica. "Putting all that stuff in there."

She tumbled crossly into one side of the bed. Ann, however, glided over to the window. It was a paler dark-ness out there. Strange. No streets, no buildings. Yet a world in motion as the wind tore at trees.

"It's nice having company," mumbled Jessica from the bed. "I don't believe I could have done it if there hadn't been someone to come with."

She yawned, feeling that far more than one day's events had taken place since last she slept. The bed was strange, the room was strange, the people were not a bit like her own, but there were no sirens wailing, no flares, no bombs.

Over at the window Ann wondered what it must be like for her mother this evening, coming back from work to an empty house. They had said goodbye at first light on the pummiced doorstep.

"You'll be all right," the woman said. "If things get worse here I'll come and join you, I promise. If they get better you'll be back in no time at all."

Then she kissed her daughter and said: "Got your handkerchief?"

Ann nodded.

"I'll wave to you when you're half-way down the street. Don't turn round until you get that far."

Her mother had fluttered her hanky, a large old one of her father's. But Ann, with both hands filled with luggage, couldn't rescue hers from her pocket. So she'd nodded her head vigorously instead, then turned and gone on to the end of the row. At the corner she'd set down her case and waved her arm. The white handkerchief was fluttering away like a little flame, and still it fluttered as Ann turned the corner.

"You know," said Jessica from under the bedclothes, "you can't help seeming odd at times, with your father being dead. But I'd rather be here with you than with any of the others."

After this generous tribute Jessica glided blissfully into sleep.

20

3

"Sorry I'm late, Mam," sang Gwyneth Jones. "That's been a day."

Mrs. Jones had half her head in the oven, getting her daughter's tea. Fair proud they were of the girl. In a man's world she was now, school teaching.

"We've been sorting evacuees," called Gwyneth, kicking off her shoes. "There's a relief."

She was feeling the glow of work well done. She'd beaten those men at their job, getting the three youngsters billeted as near enough together as made no difference. It just needed a bit of initiative on someone's part.

"I ended up with three kids in Pengaron."

Mrs. Jones appeared at the kitchen door, her homely face red from cooking and with a kind of shining surprise about her.

"What did you say?" she asked.

"Pengaron, Mam."

"You've never been billeting youngsters there?"

"Why shouldn't we indeed?"

"That is not a place to be taking them."

"Mam," said Gwyneth Jones, "forget about the musty old legends and tell me straight why we shouldn't billet evacuees in Pengaron if there are homes will have them."

"Because — " said Mrs. Jones, and then stopped. There were things she didn't have words for. Her daughter had words because she'd been trained in them. But to dismiss people's beliefs as musty old legends. . .

"Come on Mam. If I've done something wrong I want to know what it is."

"Oh dear," said Mrs. Jones. "You know quite well they'll be the only ones there, until — "

21

"So what? It will cheer the old place up."

"It hasn't worked in the past."

"Well," said Gwyneth calmly, "there are three youngsters sleeping there this evening, so we'll soon find out if it works this time."

"But — "

"Mam, we're in the twentieth century. In the middle of a war, remember. We've got to let old superstitions rest."

"There won't be another this side of Duffryn for them to talk to."

"They have each other. That is what they wanted. That is why I have taken them there."

"Well," said Mrs. Jones, "well — "

And there was a kind of surprise remaining in her all evening that her daughter just could not get at.

"They're all very curious about us," said Ann as she noticed how the inhabitants of Pengaron eyed them hard first and welcomed them second.

Jessica was still puzzling over words she had caught on waking at early dawn. Mr. Pincher was just going off to work and his voice carried in the quiet cottage:

"Don't you be worrying over them youngsters. They're strangers to the place. And big at that. They won't be affected, you'll see."

Affected by what? Jessica wondered. And why should their being strangers make a difference?

They were welcomed, without a doubt. As soon as the carrier in the village heard that the girls would be attending the school in Duffryn when it opened after the summer holiday he offered straightway to take them along in his van to have a look at the place.

"Think I'll explore," said Peter meanwhile, his nose sniffing the air with relish. The sea couldn't be all that far away. The Captain had gone off that morning with a click of the latch and a stooping of his great frame in the doorway. With him went a load of fishing tackle, and

22

Peter knew that a day of independence stretched ahead.

He began by establishing some acquaintance with Pengaron.

"Staying with the Captain?" quizzed Evan Thomas. He did most of the running-around work at the post-office, while his mother sat behind the counter as she had done for forty odd years, like Mahomet's mountain.

"An evacuee staying with the Captain," said Evan raising his voice for the benefit of the mountain who looked severely along her quarried nose.

"There will be no children staying long in Pengaron," she snapped. Her mouth closed like the blocking of a pass in front of the astonished boy.

Peter's next stop was the grocer's run by Timothy Hughes and his young wife.

"You must be from the Captain's," said the bright young man.

"Not the Captain," giggled Barbara Hughes. "There's a one."

She blushed through thick russet hair, her expanded waist-line indicating clearly that she would soon be giving birth.

"It's nice having youngsters around," said Timothy with an encouraging grin. "They don't go in for kids in these parts, seems. Not until we have them that is."

He gave his wife a wink and a nod and she giggled once more.

"Why don't they?" Peter asked directly.

"That's something they don't talk much about. Especially to us. We're recent here ourselves. Seems our baby, when he or she arrives — this week, next week — will offend against their customs."

"They're just afraid," said Barbara Hughes. "It's so long since any child's been born here. But the place fell lucky for us. Tim wasn't fit enough for the army. It meant we'd be getting married straightaway."

"You wouldn't know the history of the area then?" said Peter.

"Try Evan Thomas," said Timothy. "He's had years in the village. Not as a boy of course. Came as a man. His mam clings to him so hard, she does, makes you wonder why she wouldn't have him with her before."

"You mean *he* didn't grow up here?"

"As I say," said Timothy, "they don't go in for having kids around. They've tried already, nicely of course, to persuade us to leave. But we're determined, aren't we, that our baby'll shake them all."

"Nicely determined," said his wife and laughed again.

"Rum," said Peter as he went out of the store. Whatever happened to all the rooted families old Turtle said you would find in villages?

He decided against going back to the post office for a chat with Evan while the Mountain was looking on. Instead he took the lane out of Pengaron and turned down the road in the opposite direction from Duffryn.

After walking steadily for half an hour, sniffing at the air as he went, Peter emerged at the top of a rocky incline. At its foot, pitted with boulders, was the beach. All the things that had ever mattered in his life fell into insignificance beside this. The tide had gone well out, but not past the strips of rocky coast which protruded to the far right and the far left. He was standing exactly at the centre of a bay.

The varied cliff formation was the most impressive thing, more so because it was intensely poised against the free-flowing elements of air and water. Peter scanned it slowly. Halfway along the bay's northern arm the land bellied out into what looked like the beginnings of a round tower.

The boy's gaze was held by it. Then something fluttered from a nearer part of the beach, causing him with reluctance to take his eyes off the dark turret.

Slightly to the south of where he stood was a huge spread of rock with pinnacle peaks. It arose a good way out on the open beach and flocks of gulls were wheeling and settling from above. But it wasn't the gulls that had drawn his attention, Peter was sure.

Nothing else, however, moved now, and the boy considered what he might do next. Beneath a low quilt of cloud strong light had built in the south where the sun ought to be but due west the sea was sable.

It was clearly not the weather for bathing, but he could walk among shells and snails and seaweed; he could prize a few limpets and see if there was a crab around or a jelly fish; he could search rock pools and generally beachcomb. The sort of thing, he said to himself, that girls don't like.

Peter scrambled down the incline. He'd never had a stretch of sand so entirely to himself. Perhaps it wasn't a good place for bathing, with all those rocks around. Or perhaps people didn't come because of the war. There wouldn't be other kids here in any case, to share the place with.

Peter gave a sudden whoop of delight and ran, it didn't matter where. He was coming up to the pinnacle rock when a man's form broke from the shade. Peter stopped. The man must be walking backwards and forwards for he kept emerging out of shadow and then disappearing. The strange thing about him, though, was the cloak he was wearing.

The man looked across at Peter and the boy had the oddest sensation that things had shifted, that the dark rough cloak belonged elsewhere, that the breeze was colder and the sand soggier under his feet. Yet the place had not changed: the sea was still the sea and the rock as wrinkled and grey as ever.

Peter shook off the feeling. Probably just some fisherman in a cape, waiting for a companion to join him. Peter turned away and just as his attention had been drawn to the rock from the black cliff at the north end of the bay, so he found that his gaze now reverted to the round turret.

"I'll go there," he said on the spur of the moment. One glance at the whereabouts of the tide told him there was still time to cross the beach. He could always return by land.

As he went he had an uncanny feeling that he was all the time being watched from the shadow of the pinnacle rock. He wouldn't look back, he determined. Gradually the mound itself put all suspicion out of his head.

It was growing as he approached. The thought of a fortress had occurred to Peter but the shape seemed to arise naturally from the rock as if wind and weather had been its only creators.

His awe of the place was increasing also. Viewed from a distance, it had seemed to lie fairly low, but its great girth had deceived the eye. Besides, it had a kind of brooding presence that sucked you close but offered no admittance. Peter found that he could circumnavigate the needle rocks at its foot and might even attempt the lower slopes that gave some foothold, but the tower itself was impregnably smooth.

He went round trying to find a path to the cliff top. Strangely difficult compared with the other part of the bay. Everything brought him back to the same smooth rock. Eventually he went north, past it, in the teeth of the oncoming tide. There he found narrow gritty footholds by which he could pull himself up to the headland. A little to his right were the upper reaches of the great circle.

"Oh," gasped Peter.

What had promised to be a complete turret viewed from the beach was hideously shattered on the landward side. A magnificent shell it stood, strong but purposeless; stone sprawling in all directions except for the curve that faced the sea.

You could tell how the circle should have gone. There were stubs of rock at intervals and if he stepped between these Peter reckoned he would be in the original —

The word wouldn't come. What was it that had stood there?

Peter drew near. Once he was inside he could look over

the parapet. Why was he delaying like this? Why didn't he just go forward as he wanted to? The rock itself was drawing him.

That was why, Peter suddenly thought. Part of him was struggling against the pull of the place. He clung to a section of rock as he passed, though his feet were still moving. They were carrying him on through the gap. One foot had touched an inner slab of stone. He had the sensation of sea coming up over him and washing him away. With great gasps Peter held on.

"I'm not," he panted " — not going there — "

Some invisible power threw him hard against the rock so that his shins were scraped, then tried dragging him forward into what remained of the tower's ring.

There was such a hum in his ears that Peter only distantly heard the sea as it washed into the bay. The tide was sending inch by inch a further trickle of brine in the direction of the mound. As the water broke round its base, the rock's power gave way. Peter found he could relax his hold and stand up.

The world wheeled round to normal. Ahead, the white speckled waves rolled joyously forward. Above, gulls were giving short sharp sounds like the all-clear siren.

The place would have welcomed him quietly now, but Peter jerked abruptly from it, choosing rather to descend the slope onto more fertile ground, following rutted bicycle tracks until he came to a path that led back to the bay's centre.

"It wasn't a fisherman's cape," Peter said aloud as he made his way home. "It *was* a man in a cloak."

4

"Have you always lived in Pengaron?" asked Peter.

Mrs. Pincher relaxed a little in the midst of her work. She had been happy to get the girls out of the house but she didn't mind so much having Peter around.

"Not quite always, Peter *bach*," she said. "I was a young bride when I came to these parts. My husband got employment with the farmers down by here. The last hedger's wife was expecting a child and they were for moving out before it was born. So with the cottage empty — "

It struck Peter that he had heard a similar tale at the grocer's.

"Did you never have any children?" he asked casually.

Mrs. Pincher's mouth tightened.

"Nearly," she said. "Twice. One never got born, and the other died of pneumonia within three weeks. The doctor said: 'Cold here in the winter. Not the climate for it.' But I have known none better in my life. The youngsters were growing up in coal dust in the Rhondda."

"Will Barbara Hughes be having a baby soon?" asked Peter.

"Maybe she will — maybe she won't."

"But I thought — "

"She is expecting one," said Mrs. Pincher.

Peter tried another tack.

"I suppose there're people who've lived in the village all their lives. Old Mrs. Thomas at the post office — "

"This place knew Blodwen Thomas before the last war," said Mrs. Pincher. "She was here when we came. But not always. Not in Pengaron."

"Wasn't her son brought up in the village?"

"Evan? Oh, that lad was born on a visit to her parents in

Shropshire. Stayed there too he did. Went to school over by there. His Da had an accident and Pengaron was lonely without others to play with. He visited his Mam during holidays of course. Came to help her then after his other relatives passed on. She leans on him now so's his life's not his own."

"There must be children around. . .on the farms. . . ?"

Mrs. Pincher glanced at him in a curious way.

"Not on the farms in Pengaron," she said. "Not staying that is. Rees the Sheep has a couple of sons. Twins they are. But they go to school away from here."

"Why don't they go to school in Duffryn?"

"Plenty of youngsters for that on the far side of the line," said Mrs. Pincher briskly. "It is a small school, though. Not like yours in Aber, Peter *bach*. But it is homely and the girls will like it."

She leant forward to clean the oven and talked staccato between the flails of her arm about household activities.

"There was a man on the beach wearing a cloak," said Peter suddenly.

Mrs. Pincher's arm slowed.

"Walking up and down. Waiting for someone I suppose. He didn't *look* like a fisherman."

"Odd like? Cracked?"

The arm, Peter saw, was almost at a standstill.

"I didn't mean that. It was just the cloak you see."

"Cloak — ?"

"And he was hanging around. And vanishing."

"Vanishing — ?"

"I thought p'raps you'd know him — he might live round here?"

"None as I know of," said Mrs. Pincher, and the arm went vigorously into motion again.

It was as well, Peter thought, that Ann and Jessica should appear at that moment. He addressed them swiftly:

"*Bore da*."

"Proper Welsh you are getting, Peter *bach*."

29

"Let's have a walk," Peter said.

Jessica was ready to bolt. The sight of Mrs. Pincher at the incessant cleansing of her home was like pins in her flesh.

"*Why* aren't there other kids in Pengaron?" asked Peter as soon as they pulled away from the cottages. "It's near the sea. You'd think the place would be invaded with holiday-makers — getting away from the bombs for a bit."

"Perhaps they send them away to school," suggested Ann.

"You bet they do. Those that exist at all. Send them away to live as well. None of them are around even in the holidays."

"There must be plenty in Abertowyn," said Jessica. "They can't all be evacuees. And in Duffryn too. Enough for the school."

"That's the point," said Peter. "There are children everywhere except in Pengaron."

"There's us."

"We're only here by accident. We weren't intended to come."

"You mean there's a mystery about the place."

"I'll say there is. And it's the older ones create it. Like old Ma Thomas or your Mrs. Pincher."

"I know," said Jessica. "The Pinchers keep turning the wireless down when we go into the room."

"That's nothing," said Ann quickly. "They don't want us to hear if there's been more bombing."

"They won't talk about things," said Jessica, "that Mummy would talk about all the time."

But Peter was frowning.

"There are other matters," he hinted darkly.

"Tell us," said Ann.

"I don't know that I can, but there was the oddest chap on the beach. . . ."

That evening Jessica hovered on the tiny landing above the open living room where Mr. and Mrs. Pincher sat quietly together. She would have said, if accused of eavesdropping, that you could hear most things easily enough anyway in the cottage. The Pinchers' voices were low, however, and Jessica was lending some aid to the situation.

"I tell you," she heard Mrs. Pincher say, "it is beginning again. I should never have kept them here. I should never have let that modern young busybody bring them into my home."

"What harm but your own fears?" replied a gruffer voice. "What can touch three healthy youngsters? A sickly babe, maybe — "

"The boy saw him today."

"Saw — "

"*Him*. The one in the cloak. Over by the big rock, he said. Who else but him?"

"I wouldn't have believed it," said the man.

"You believe me now, though?"

"I am not saying so."

"He comes early, that one. And always to bring disaster."

"Listen, woman. Have I ever said it was anything but nonsense? It's the way the rock's shadow falls. The shape of it — "

" — comes always as a warning."

"Tush. You women go on making mountains — "

"It is we who have known the loss."

"Perhaps," said her husband slowly, "it is not these ones from the city that do this. That bring it back to you."

"No," and now Mrs. Pincher's voice was taking on an unusual and intense passion. "It is Hughes' young wife, I know, seeking to bring her child into the world in such a spot as this. I tell her what will happen. There will be no child expected this day month. And no child in her arms neither."

"You remember the past too much," groaned the man. "It is a new generation growing up. They will not have the same fate as us."

"It has always been the same, I tell you. When you have

31

been hurted as I have — It's myself I see when I look at Hughes' wife. Myself five and twenty years — "

"Jessica," hissed Ann.

"Sh!"

Jessica was forced to draw back into the bedroom.

The next morning all three children set out for the beach. What weirdness had seemed to exist by lamplight was dispelled in the freshness of day. If there was a tightness about Mrs. Pincher's expression both Ann and Jessica could put it down to her discovery of their intrusion into the wardrobe. Last night the door had been locked and the key removed.

"We ought to mention it," Ann had suggested, wishing that Jessica would agree to own up.

But Mrs. Pincher's prim silence on the subject had made Jessica more defiant still and the moment passed with misunderstanding on both sides.

"She wants us out of the house," Jessica fretted. "The Pinchers don't like us here."

Day, however, made a difference: the countryside was at its ripest. At the same time the earliest tints of autumn were just beginning to flush through the summer green; birds were descending on hazel and rowan and elderberry; the air carried its message of impending change.

The children left the stony track and crossed through gorse and burweed to mount the undulating land. The grass was thick enough to spring them away from any wetness in the soil.

"Landmarks," declared Jessica, pointing to trees. They passed oaks and beeches with spreading, witch-like roots, and sycamores which gripped straight into the ground with huge elephant toes.

Jessica was one of the best runners in her school and felt magic in her feet when she touched grass. She rambled more than the other two, jumping high under branches to experience their green shade. It was different with Ann.

32

She went tortoise-like, watching the ground for pitfalls.

"Shall we go down?" she panted finally, her leg muscles aching.

They descended at a run into a morass of nettly grass.

"Ugh!" screeched Jessica, jumping like a goat.

Peter reflected, not for the first time, what a difference girls made to any expedition.

They came out into the bay, whipped playfully by wind and exhilarated by sun and waves and scudding clouds.

"Isn't it tremendous!" exclaimed Jessica, willing for once just to stand still and look.

"You know," said Peter as they stood swallowing great gusts of air, "old Turtle's good on invasions. We did all about them last year. They nearly all came from the east so this part of Britain was the last stand."

"Was it captured?"

"Occupied!" It was a word familiar to all of them from the daily papers.

Ann pictured invaders coming up silently along river banks; flames burst open the dark as an unwitting town-stead was fired; shadows engaged one another.

"Have you noticed," she said, "how they were all following the sun when they came this way. Perhaps they were afraid it would disappear and they'd always be left in the dark."

Jessica yawned.

"Mummy says sea air makes you feel tired."

"Let's go down," said Peter.

They descended to the beach. Ann looked across the bay to the dark circular cliff. Peter gave it merely a glance and turned away. He pointed to the craggy rock that rose resplendent on the foreshore.

"That's where we're going," he said.

They picked their way among rock and scree out to the open sand. The sun was strengthening and ahead of them a whole pathway of smashed shell glittered like white glass. Peter raided a pile of seaweed and went to slap Jessica's

33

back with a string of wet rubbery berries.

"Ugh!" she screeched, and ran off.

He gave a great shout of triumph and ran too, holding his seaweed at arm's length, shaking it as a dread invader would shake his spear. Jessica danced away, skirting the trickling inlets that the tide had left. Ann came to a sudden stop.

She was squinting into the sun's brightness. A man's shape had detached itself from the shadow of the rock. His outline quivered so much against the light that it wasn't until he came close that she could tell he was wearing a cloak. At the same time the sea's note changed. There was something harsher and colder about the breeze which made the other two stop in their tracks. For a moment the man had seemed like a reflection in water but now he appeared clearly and solidly before them. Jessica noticed straightaway how blue his eyes were.

He called to them: "My name is Duguth. Follow me over to Gullzin — " and he pointed to the rock. "There are others waiting to greet you."

He turned and walked ahead as if certain of their answer. The children looked at one another.

"It's where we're going," said Peter. "We'll find out now."

They crossed the sand to the mass of ascending crags. Gullzin was clearly a last perch for birds in the incoming tides and a first one when the sea turned back. No birds had settled there today, however, for three old men had mounted the sides of the rock and were squatting in crannies like hermit crabs. They all seemed to be cloaked in the same dark fashion.

Duguth stopped and waited for the children to catch up. Then they heard him say to his companions:

"The three who will perform the task for us have come."

Jessica shrank when she saw the old men. One was wizened and one was hawk-nosed and all had eyes greedy as birds. The one who was neither wizened nor hawk-nosed came down from his perch. He walked round the children

34

as if picking up some peculiar scent from them. Then he addressed himself to Duguth.

"What do they know?"

"I have explained nothing," said Duguth. "Yet I saw the boy shudder when he turned from looking at Caer Owen."

Ann took off her glasses and tried to rub away the salt that had misted them. She wanted to observe Duguth as closely as she could.

"If he is afraid already he will be no good for the task," said the old man as if Peter were not at hand listening.

"It is harder to bridle the horse after it has been kicked," said Duguth, "but it is often done."

"They are weak-looking," screeched the wizened one peering down at Ann and Jessica.

"They are necessary," said Duguth.

"Well," said the old man who had walked round the children, "as you say, the children who are necessary have at last come."

He turned once more to gaze at the three with a look that seemed to long for some of their youthfulness.

"Come," said Duguth to the children. "We will walk a little."

He directed them to accompany him along the beach.

"You did not understand, I know," said Duguth. "But *something* you understood. We have need of you. It is the reason for our meeting here today."

He glanced across to the other side of the bay.

"Your war has drawn our destinies very close."

He turned and looked at Peter as if threading his attention. Then he moved his gaze once more over to the black mound and Peter followed it.

"There is a task for the boy Peter to perform."

Peter closed his eyes for the mound was suddenly more than it had been. With the light full upon it, it had the explosive radiance of jet. He stood with his eyes shut, seeing and not seeing. He felt again how his body had been hurled against rock.

35

"No," he said fiercely and defiantly. "I won't."

He opened his eyes and kept them fixed on Duguth, refusing to look again over the bay.

"We have to go now," he said. "It's been interesting talking to you but we really can't stay any longer. We're expected back."

He veered swiftly towards land and the girls instinctively followed.

"Stop," called Duguth.

His voice had power to halt them but they did not immediately turn.

"When you discover that you are bound by the circle, come back to me here."

The breeze from the sea dropped a little but the voice did not sound again. Ann turned at last and gazed across the deserted beach toward the pinnacle rock where gulls had settled in a throng.

"I wish," she thought, "I had *seen* him go."

When they reached home they found that Miss Jones had called. Peter's school was to meet the next day to sort out arrangements on the new premises before term started. That meant a journey into Abertowyn. Miss Jones was prepared as a special treat to take all three children into town with her.

"I'm to go along as a billeting officer in any case," she said.

Mrs. Pincher gave her a hard, straight look. She hadn't

forgotten that this carefree young woman had left the billeting of Peter to herself.

"The girls won't want to be going," she said disapprovingly. "Not to town. *We* are not going there very often."

Miss Jones understood that Mrs. Pincher regarded busy towns with cinemas and traffic as potentially sinful.

"That's all right," she said determinedly. "This lot won't be getting out of their depth."

Mrs. Pincher's doubts, however, remained until next morning when Huw Pincher remarked:

"Good thing you are sending them to Aber for the day. That is not a newspaper for them to be seeing."

Later, as the girls made their bed, Jessica said: "She's letting us go just to get rid of us. Did you notice there was no front page on that paper today? I suppose it means more air raids. I do wish the Pinchers would let us *know*."

When Miss Jones met them at Duffryn station she also showed that she had registered Mrs. Pincher's disapproval.

"No gas masks?" she called as they tumbled off the bus. "There's a nice thing."

"We didn't think," said Ann.

"Mrs. Pincher should have thought. I wonder what she's about, letting you up to town without them."

"We're not going to be bombed here, are we?" asked Peter.

"It is better to do things right from the start," said Miss Jones in her bossiest fashion. "You will have to carry them in to school each day."

She relaxed, however, once they were on the train and steaming down into Abertowyn. It lay, she told them, on an estuary, central to a farming community in one direction and a colliery in another. Abertowyn College, which Peter and his mates were to share, was the pride of the area. It had a pillared entrance surmounted by a coat-of-arms. Before the war it had added stained glass to its hall windows. Now, alas, its usual additions were pink brick air-raid shelters with sand-bagged mouths.

As they passed through the last sidings of coal trucks, Peter asked:

"Why aren't there any other children in Pengaron?"

"We hadn't thought of billeting — "

"I mean why aren't there any *growing up* there?"

"You've noticed, have you? Fables," said Miss Jones. "Accidents. What not."

"What sort of accidents?"

"Oh, babies not surviving. People think the place has a curse on it."

"Is it true?" asked Ann.

"Never in this wide world," said Gwyneth Jones, raising her hands in dramatic horror, "will you have me believe such a thing. Superstition, that is, you see. Comes with the country and not having electricity."

From the station Miss Jones walked her charges briskly uphill towards a busy thoroughfare. She lodged Peter at a bus stop while she took Ann and Jessica down more placid streets into a square flanked by a small museum and library. There were benches, pigeons, and flower beds.

"Nice and quiet it is, here," she said. "You can eat your sandwiches in peace. Have a wander round the museum when you feel like it. Peter and I will join you at three o'clock. We'll get dinner at school. But you'll be able to amuse yourselves all right, won't you."

"Oh yes," said Jessica brightening with a new thought. "We could look round the shops."

Gwyneth Jones hesitated for a fraction of a second while she glanced down at them. At Ann, like a serious little owl, with drooping hem line and black laced shoes. At Jessica, pale-cheeked and lanky, her thick hair restrained into plaits. Evacuees, thought Miss Jones, always had a tamed and shabby look about them. No, she was certain these two would attract no trouble.

"I'll tell you how to get there," she said.

After she had gone the girls went on standing as if confined by an invisible cage. Both were aware that Mrs. Pincher would not approve of their present position. Alone in a public square of an unfamiliar town. Jessica kicked one foot idly against the other.

"Shall we eat?"

They were carrying Mrs. Pincher's neat little packets of food.

"It's a bit early," said Ann. "Let's look in the museum first."

"Don't fancy it," said Jessica.

The building was imposing and adult-like and would take effort to come to terms with.

"Let's wander over, anyway."

They passed beds of asters and begonias beside one of which was a group of stone figures. A man on a plinth had twisted his body energetically in the performance of some sport. DISKOBOLUS — THE DISCUS THROWER was inscribed at the bottom. A metal plate told them that this stone copy of the famous Greek bronze was presented by some Alderman in 1920.

There had been another artist at work, though, who had added a flamboyant setting. Four exuberant fauns flanked the plinth, their feet descending into plant tendrils. Half man, half goat, they guarded the athlete with grotesque humour.

"What shall we do then?" said Jessica as she and Ann gaped at the statuary and wished there had been a fountain.

"Look at the shops?"

"Mmmm."

They turned and crossed the square, cutting back into the centre of traffic. It was a busy and noisy time of day. Buses and lorries lumbered round bends. On the pavements people were staggering in all directions to avoid contact.

The girls stopped for a few entranced moments outside a cinema that was showing the latest Tarzan adventure. A collection of stuffed jungle animals littered the foyer.

The main shopping centre crossed at right angles the road that had brought them uphill from the station. As they were waved over by a traffic policeman with his arms banded in white, they caught sight of the familiar red frontage that was Woolworths and turned happily in the direction of counters they could wander round as they pleased.

Outside they ran into an old school acquaintance who had travelled in the same party of evacuees: Patsy Doyle with ginger ringlets and china-doll eyes.

"Jethica," she squeaked, more loudly than a passing truck.

"Patsy," exclaimed Jessica who liked above all things to have people look pleased to see her.

Ann reared backwards like a horse restrained too fast.

"Ithn't that marvellouth!" said Patsy, and the three of them went round Woolworths together.

"I think I'll look at that museum," said Ann when they got back to the door.

Patsy didn't squeal this time but she stared at Ann with eyes extraordinarily glazed.

"You can't do that," declared Jessica. "We're together."

"You can meet me there at dinner time," Ann said determinedly. "Just outside. See you later, Patsy."

Ann raced the last few yards to the museum, skirting the ridiculous fauns. All the time she'd been going round the shops her mind had been straying to this place. She went slowly up the steps and inside.

The area was rich in Roman encampments so that local digs had yielded a great deal. There were casefuls of pottery, coins, and statuettes. Then as Ann moved into another room she found herself dropping back by a thousand years into an age of bronze. Large cooking utensils, agricultural tools and primitive weapons declared a harsher, tribal existence.

She reached the last room in which an elderly attendant

sat peacefully sucking a sweet. Maps and charts decorated the walls. Ann peered conscientiously at a range of crinkled skin and parchment. The earliest ones were written in a language that she guessed must be Latin.

In spite of their variable outline the maps all seemed to be about this part of Wales. One, dated 1917, had names Ann could recognise. Abertowyn. Porthglas. That was a railway track connecting them. She could even make out Duffryn in very small print. And *Pengaron*.

Ann was pleased and began to work back among the older charts. Some of the places were still there, under more ancient names. Abertowyn was a Roman settlement. There was more shading now to suggest wooded areas, and where Pengaron should have been was covered by one of these.

On several of the maps was a faintly inked, curved line, running from one arm of Pengaron bay to take in a sweep of countryside and emerge along the other arm of the bay.

The area was shaded on the earliest map to look like forest. The line appeared again, however, in a later period where no shading existed. And finally on the map for 1917 it was marked as a ring of proposed excavation.

Ann went backwards and forwards along the wall. Perhaps Miss Jones could help in reading those details on the early maps: she probably understood Latin. For the line excited Ann.

Hadn't Duguth said: "When you discover that you are bound by the circle — " Well, it wasn't a complete circle, but that was only because of the sea.

6

When they reached home the girls found to their surprise that a fire had been lit in the Pinchers' cottage. There was also a new presence in the room. Mrs. Pincher was, with unexpected tenderness, fussing over her brother. He was a miner come to spend a few days where the air might do his lungs good. You could see before he stood up that the man was sick.

"Bore da," he said, rising to shake hands. "A pleasure it is. . . . Beth here tells me you are more than a step from home."

The man's voice had grit in it, striking into sudden flashes of warmth.

"Don't you disturb yourself, Glyn," said his sister. "These two can manage. A great help they can be when they are wanting."

The sallow-cheeked man sank quietly back into the chair. When Huw Pincher arrived from work he too yielded his usual comforts at the fender to his guest. The small room glowed like an oven. They drew up round the table. The tea, thicker and darker than the girls had ever seen it before, flowed sputtering from the teapot.

"Worst thing they ever did," said Glyn Evans, "was finding them coal seams. We would all have been better off hunting seals and burning their fat to warm our feet."

"It is something," said Mrs. Pincher, "to be clear of coal dust. Too much washing and scrubbing there was."

"It is a beautiful country here, and a fine job you got, Huw, man," said Glyn Evans. "Being above ground, in the open air. There is many a man would cough worse than I do to get that.'

"Is it — " said Jessica, and stopped abashed as all eyes turned on her.

"Yes, Jessica," said Glyn. "It is, fine. Ask away."

"It must be very dark down the mine."

"Black as old Harry it is," said Glyn. "You take lamps with you down the coal face, but that might be miles after you set out."

"Then you've a long walk."

"Crawl too," said Glyn. "Always warm it is there. You are needing no clothes."

"But it must hurt," said Ann, "if you are crawling among coal."

"The scars are always there," said Glyn. "What miner is without them?"

Jessica fixed her eyes on Mrs. Pincher's dresser with its assortment of willow-pattern plates dating from her wedding day. An ornament of a crinolined lady fastened her attention. Immersed in the world of this little aristocrat she drew comfort to herself.

"Jessica," said Mrs. Pincher, "there's enough to eat, is it?"

Jessica blushed, brought back from her attempt to escape this terrible world of scars and darkness.

"Our neighbour's made us an offer," said Mrs. Pincher. "Said this morning. Glyn here would get better air in his boat. Mind now you say 'yes'. A strange man in some of his ways is the Captain but he's been good to us with the fish."

The Captain in fact not only stood to his word but he included Peter in the invitation.

"I won't invite you girls this time," he told Ann and Jessica. "Sea fishing can be a bit rough when you've not done it before."

"That's all right," said Ann who thought driving hooks into fishes' mouths a very rough sport indeed.

Jessica didn't know whether to be disappointed or not, but she was determined to bait the Captain a little.

"I suppose," she said, "if you don't *want* us. . ."

The Captain placed his huge hand on her head and gave it a shake.

"There are no privies aboard boat you know," he said. At which Jessica was stunned into silence.

"Ask the Captain if he's got a map," Ann whispered to Peter.

"Of what?"

"Pengaron. And round about."

"All right," said Peter, glowing with the prospect of a fishing trip.

A map of the area proved no difficulty, for the Captain had a chestful of charts. Ann pored over it after she and Jessica had gone upstairs for the night. Then she sketched her own version and put in the line she remembered from the museum maps.

"You see it went from here — to here — and *nearly* touched Duffryn — I remember that," she said, forcing Jessica to take an interest.

The line swept inland in a deep arc, beginning and ending at the opposite corners of Pengaron bay. Miss Jones had been helpful. "Wolves," she'd declared about one chart. "A danger zone probably."

The area for excavation in 1917 she had known nothing about. "It didn't happen," she said. "Probably the war made them abandon it."

Jessica came up close behind Ann.

"You know," she said, "it's exactly like a crescent moon."

Peter's pulse raced as they reached the coast. He had the courage now to look across to the dark mound and to point it out to the Captain. The man's bushy eyebrows shot up.

"Been *there*, have you?" he said. "The place draws you, I'll admit."

"Does it have a name?"

"Indeed. They call it Caer Owen."

The Captain pronounced it slowly and darkly. Peter recalled the last time he had heard the words spoken.

"*Caer* means a fortified place," said Glyn Evans.

"Who was Owen?"

The Captain shrugged.

"It's a common enough name in these parts. Probably nothing to do with what was there originally. The Welsh like the personal touch."

"You're not Welsh, are you?" said Peter.

"No sir," said the Captain. "I was born in a ship going round the coast of New Zealand. I've lived in both the east and the west but I married a Welsh wife in the end. That's why I'm here now. And it'll be my last berth on this side of things."

"I didn't think you sounded Welsh."

"Did you not, Peter *bach*?" said the Captain. "I'll tell you what, when you travel as much as I have you become a bit of everything. And when you're everything it's as good as being nothing."

Peter felt he had never met anyone who was less like Nothing than the Captain. The man had the power of rocks. Of Caer Owen.

The Captain took them a long way south round the bay, then down to a stone breakwater harbour and a collection of small craft. His own boat was flat-bottomed with blistered paintwork and an out-board motor. Between them he and Peter hauled the ropes and tackle aboard, for the Captain insisted that Glyn Evans should put no strain on himself until the fishing demanded it.

The girls got off the bus before it reached Duffryn. They had come to the main road that ran on endlessly in each direction beside the railway line.

"You know," said Jessica, "if that old track does still exist it's probably buried under this road."

They passed some cottages on their way to the station. There was a wicket gate that was a well-known short cut over the rails into the station building and then into Duffryn itself. Today it was closed and everything was quiet.

A notice pinned to the gate said that a goods train had been derailed further down the line. There would be no more trains passing through Duffryn that day. The station keeper had obviously taken the opportunity to close his gates and have a holiday. People must go round by the bridge if they wanted to enter the village.

They walked on automatically, Jessica hoping to beguile Ann into abandoning her trail and entering the village instead. She remembered from their visit to see the school that there was a flea-pit cinema in Duffryn and shops. . . . Jessica fingered the pound note her father had slipped into her pocket before she came away.

They were passed by cyclists and a couple of farm waggons. The road ran between stone walls and telegraph poles, signifying that semi-inhabited territory that borders major human settlements. *Duffryn* meant *valley* they'd been told, and over on the far side was a range of quiet and meditative hills.

"When I was very very little," said Jessica, "I remember living near a railway line. Mummy didn't like it much. You could look right over from the upstairs windows and there were lots of lines crossing. The trains always slowed down as they passed and you could wave to them. I thought the rails were a kind of sea or space or something. I thought I'd never be able to find out what people were like on the other side."

The waggon swaying in front turned at right angles but by the time the girls came up to the bridge the road was clear. It was a short span over a bed of gleaming rails. A row of cottages on the farther side stood with their shoulders to the crossing.

Jessica stubbed her toe hard on something and screeched, hopping wildly back.

"There's nothing there," said Ann peering down. "But — I don't think we want to go that way."

"I just thought," said Jessica, "that we might have a peep into the village. There's a shop — "

46

Ann was no longer listening. She had raised her arms and was holding them out in front as if she was feeling for something. Jessica stepped forward until she was in line with her, facing the bridge, and she too extended her arms. Then she snorted.

"Ann, what are we playing at? Feeling for nothing."

"Something," said Ann in hushed tones, "is touching me."

Jessica turned and stared disbelievingly at her rapt face. Ann felt it impossible to explain the sensation she had of air moving in little currents, coiling and whorling against her skin. It was with her as she moved across the entry to the bridge. When she tried to push onto the bridge, however, it rebuffed her and she halted, trembling.

Jessica was watching like a bewildered dog. She went nearer to the bridge than Ann and still could feel nothing disturbing. One more step and she was almost at the place where she had stubbed her toe.

"Come on," she called, "there's absolutely nothing — "

Something hard came up against her shoulder. When she put out her hands to counter it a rough and flashing surface appeared momentarily and then as her fingers moved on returned to invisibility. Jessica stretched her arms as far as she could. The whole of the bridge's entry was filled with some kind of barrier that was clear and faceted like the crystal stones her mother kept in her jewel box.

Jessica dropped her arms and watched the brilliant stone fade from view. She was looking through clear air at the bridge with its parapet and cottages and trees. Nothing appeared to prevent their crossing.

Ann moved involuntarily on, keeping beside a low stone wall that protected the railway embankment. Every now and then Jessica saw her sway as if responding to signals emanating from the wall itself.

Jessica suddenly bounded after and tried swinging a leg over the parapet. She encountered a hard crystalline barrier rising straight from the stone beneath.

They continued until the rail track swung away through open country to the right. The road was bounded now by hedges and ditches but Ann could feel, like a tight ligament running through all obstructions, the force that imprisoned them.

When the road itself dipped beyond their track the children crossed fields and climbed rises. Sometimes the power ran beside hedgerows or marked boundaries of one kind or another; on occasion it bounded narrow paths made by the constant tread of men and cattle, as if both had been channelled by the unseen into one track.

At last they came to a stream dragging slowly through sedge.

"Oh," gasped Ann gratefully, feeling affinity with all things flowing.

She looked down at her heavy shoes, clammy in this warm weather. Her mother had insisted on her bringing them because winter would come. Now she longed to get them off and dabble her feet in water.

"We can jump it all right," said Jessica.

Ann removed her shoes and socks and let the water ripple shallowly over her toes.

"It's gone," she said, so quietly that hills and trees must have strained to listen.

Jessica slipped off her sandals and splashed in beside her. Then she groped around in the air, finding she could move quite easily upstream.

"It continues on the bank," said Ann. "So the water must interrupt whatever this thing is. D'you remember in fairy stories how people could get away from witches by jumping into streams?"

They went on, Ann feeling herself held by the spinning power. They were close to a stile when she began once more to falter. Jessica went tentatively forward and stroked at the air.

"It's just another gap," said Ann. "It picks up again afterwards."

But Jessica was approaching the stile and hopping up the three steps. Before Ann could even protest, she had jumped down on the other side and was racing up the slope calling: "I can go where I please. Hurrah. I'm outside your precious circle."

At the top of the incline she had a view of a road, no doubt the one they had diverged from earlier, with a large dark copse of firs on its farther side."

"We're in the middle of nowhere here," declared Jessica when she returned to where Ann was waiting beside the stile.

They came at last to a road where a passing drover enlightened them as to their whereabouts. Porthglas lay 'up by there' and in the other direction the road would take them down into Pengaron. If they went ahead over the fields the way they were going now they would come to the sea.

Ann checked her map.

"D'you see?" she said after the man had gone on. "That's where we must be. There's the road that goes north. It's the one from the other end of Pengaron. So it means — "

She tried sketching something in.

" — that we've come round in a curve — behind Pengaron — "

"Phew," said Jessica. "I knew it was miles."

"And if we went towards the sea we'd come out here — at the top of the bay."

"But we don't have to," said Jessica quickly. "The road takes us right home."

"Duguth was right then, about our being in the circle."

"But it isn't really a circle," Jessica pointed out. "The curve's got to stop when it reaches the sea."

"The best fishing," said Captain Marks, "is out by the pinnacle rocks."

Peter could see nothing but the swell.

"If you're looking for them," said the Captain, "you will have to go under the surface. The earth there is as rocky as the land around. When fish get tired of the sandy plains they make for something more interesting where they'll have hiding places. Those are the best hunting grounds, I'm telling you. Plenty of conger there."

"Oh," said Peter, almost suffocating with excitement, "is that where we're going?"

"No," said the Captain, "not today."

"But — "

"We're not going there for several reasons," said the Captain firmly. "For one thing you need a strong stomach for those tides. And neither of you are tried boatmen as yet. So we're going to look for another kind of marking nearer to shore."

Peter opened his mouth to say stoutly that no tides would affect him, but Glyn Evans just said: "Ay, ay, skipper," and that was that.

"It's a calm day for ye," said the Captain as the waves lashed. "Keep your eyes on the birds. They'll spot the shoaling first."

Gulls began to wheel overhead.

"We'll keep upstream on 'em," said the Captain. "Then when we cast, the tide'll drift the bait down."

Peter's attention was focused on a spot ahead where turmoil was going on in feeding grounds of brit. At this point the boat's tossing pitched itself closer to his stomach. It was absolutely essential that he stop looking at that heaving tide.

He glanced round to see what land could be sighted. They must be well out to sea by now.

"There they go," called the Captain as the gulls shrieked.

With the motor silenced the boat rocked precariously at the mercy of the slapping waves. The reels were ready and the bait drifting, but Peter was no longer watching the hunt.

They *should* have been well out to sea. To the east a stretch of coast should be running in dim outline, with maybe a view of hills to the north. Yet Peter found he had made the most incredible mistake. *They were still enclosed in the prongs of the bay*. To north and south those protruding strips of land had stretched into a curve ten times more pronounced.

Peter looked at his companions, his mouth half open. The ocean was bucking and the Captain was hauling the fish aboard, silver and gasping and thick and angry. Peter's stomach rose with alarming jerks.

The Captain said: "Weather's breaking. D'you want to steer this time, boy?"

Peter could only shake his head, not understanding why the Captain didn't look round and see what was happening. Why couldn't he realise — ?

"Evans? You'll take her in?"

Glyn was unperturbed by his encounter with the sea. His lean body moved rhythmically with the tide.

"Ay, ay, skipper," he said.

There were points of colour in his thin cheeks.

"Look. Look," Peter tried to call, though no words came.

The spray had thickened, the waves rode incredibly high, and the homeward run was tumultuous.

"Fish for tea and fish for supper and fish for breakfast," sang the Captain. "It's best, you know, roasted in the open on a summer's evening."

Both men were ignoring Peter as they brought the boat back into harbour and tied up. He was looking faintly green.

"There's Gullzin showing," said the Captain, pointing to the characterful rock where the children had met the old men.

"I never noticed it before," said Glyn surprised.

"You wouldn't have. It was covered by water when we came down. At least nearly so. They say you can always see its tip at the highest tide."

"Isn't it dangerous?" asked Glyn.

"Not to fisherman hereabouts. We all know it. In any

case it lies too far in to get in the way. No boat leaving here goes toward it."

"What you call it?"

"Old Gullzin. Comes from Gull's Inn. The birds like it of course."

"Gullzin's good," said Glyn.

The land was a dizzying experience as they mounted the slope.

"We are coming to the end of summer," said Glyn. "The dark is inching in."

"Ay," said the Captain, "there's another winter to face."

Peter guessed that his mind was on the war.

"What the — "

"Your hands!" exclaimed Ann aghast.

All three of them stared down at the scorch marks on Peter's fingers.

For a time he had felt nothing at all. Ann had had to go much closer to the wall than on the previous day before she could pick up anything and Peter had walked straight up to it. For a moment Jessica expected that he would receive the same impression as she had done, of rough crystal.

Peter dusted off some of the charcoal blacking. It had been like contacting smouldering embers.

"I won't try that too often," he said.

"We must look awfully odd, hugging this wall," said Jessica.

It was Saturday, outside Duffryn. To their surprise the

52

wicket gate was once more open and people were pushing through onto the platform. The train from Porthglas to Abertowyn must be due; there were Duffryn children waiting to go into town for a last treat before the holidays ended.

Peter was continuing to stab his fingers inches from the stone.

"Don't," said Ann quickly.

"I know," he said, "but it sort of tempts."

Ann remembered how attached to the force she had become the previous day. It had weakened considerably, however, and the bridge over the rails was quite clear of obstruction.

"Let's go in the other direction," she said. "See where that leads."

It was harder now, what with the faintness of the power and the pressure of traffic on the road. Ann ambled like a snail with the wind against its horns.

"It seems to have gone," she said at last.

"Perhaps we have to cross — "

On the other side of the road a bramble hedge locked tight against any entry to the pastures beyond.

"It doesn't run alongside there," said Ann.

"Meaning — "

"Perhaps it goes through."

"If so then we're swinging round towards the coast," said Peter consulting the map.

"We can't get through this," declared Jessica. "It's a stinger."

Peter led the search for a suitable entry but found the hedge more deceptively needled than a porcupine.

"It was so clear yesterday," Ann tried to explain. "It was forcing us to follow it."

"Well it's playing hide-and-seek today."

"Perhaps we've got to fight our way through," speculated Jessica. "Like the enchanted thorns in the Sleeping Beauty story."

"People got stuck in those," Ann reminded her, "and

53

had to stay for as long as the enchantment lasted. It couldn't have been very comfortable."

"But time didn't count. I mean they didn't know, did they? Things were the same after the enchantment as they were when it began."

"What *are* you girls going on about?" demanded Peter, struggling with ubiquitous twigs. "Blast." He sucked hard at his hand.

"We ought to go back to nearer the station," said Ann, "and try again from there. That is — " she hesitated, "if we are going on."

Jessica turned and went up the road. Ann remained where she was.

"It's different, you see," she said. "We're having to look for it. It's making us decide things for ourselves."

Jessica trotted back to them.

"Aren't you well, Ann?" she called.

Peter seized the suggestion.

"We could rest for a while if you like."

Ann sighed.

"No," she said, "we'll go on if you both want to."

After that things happened quickly. Just where the brambles seemed a midnight thickness they discovered that the bushes overlapped and could in fact be separated into two plantations. A sinuous path drew them, struggling, into the field beyond.

"Oh," said Ann breathless, "it's here all right. Ever so strong."

Jessica, with sudden bounding joy at having overcome the brambles, went up to Ann's side and stretched out her hands toward the invisible boundary. As she touched, it glowed, crystal sharp and blue-tinged with coolness. Somewhere there was a fire too, within the brilliance, that gave out no heat but entered the tips of Jessica's fingers.

She let her arms fall, leaving Ann to pick up the trail.

"It's cold," said Jessica after a minute's walking, and blew into her fingers.

54

Perhaps it was not entirely the crystal that was chilling. The sun was still in view but infinitely weaker. Moreover the field was certainly a poor relation of all the others they had passed through. There were hedges barren of foliage, clumped like the jangled heads of upturned besoms. The grass had a despondent brown quality, with great patches of bare earth and splitting mud crusts.

"Those trees have shed all their leaves," said Jessica in astonishment.

Peter too was looking round and wondering. They passed elms that bore foliage only where the interlocking branches had formed a shield against the wind. Across the roots the fallen leaves lay drained and crisp and brown. They passed low, spine-leaved rowans that had their berries eaten or dropped or squeezed. Yet between Pengaron and Duffryn there had been berries that were just beginning to show among the intense greenery.

"It's like being in another season."

The girls had only light cardigans with them.

"We'd better keep going. Walking's the thing."

Jessica curled her hands up into her sleeves and skipped ahead several times. She came back suddenly, with the bounce fallen from her like the foliage from the boughs. Peter glanced across in the direction from which she had come. The hedge was a jubilee of crossed branches, shawled raggedly with a layer of green.

Jessica opened her mouth but shut it again.

"Sun's coming back," said Peter squinting up at the sky whose blue had deepened.

Their route led straight towards the hedge which, as they approached, seemed rich, green, and in its prime. There was one slight gap where the bushes broke and it was through this that Ann steered them.

Jessica wandered away again, the sun on her back making her feel better. Farther down the field a group of trees swished heavy-laden boughs to scatter shade along the grass. Jessica observed them casually. She was glad that not all of nature wintered early in these parts.

An unpredictable cloud must be crossing the sky, for the sunshine hesitated once more. Colours were muted mistily, while over at the edge of the field flourishing trees now had their roots carpeted with decaying leaves.

Jessica gasped. This time the fluctuating scene really shook her. The hedge had in a moment whittled into thin grey bracken, gapped widely enough to contain what Jessica thought she had glimpsed before, a stocky figure, seated cross-legged. In the midst of all this fallow landscape the man was a glaring object, for his vivid green clothing was practically phosphorescent.

This time Jessica stood still and looked back into the staring eyes. The man's mouth was set in a grin but the girl felt no warmth of friendliness. The greenness threw its dazzle over his hands and face, so that his skin seemed to partake of the same vivid hue, and Jessica could almost have sworn that it was a green man she was looking at.

He made not the slightest movement, and pleasantly amiable as was the look on his face, he seemed to have no intention of greeting the girl. Jessica, with a strong spirit of annoyance in her, continued to stare.

The man's face reminded her of the plaster clowns at the fair, all gaping hilariously to show what jolly fun everyone was having. Except that those faces had been grotesque, whereas the one in front of her was odd because it was *more symmetrical* than most.

"Jessica."

It was Peter's voice, hallooing from a distance.

"Jess— "

He must be able to see her quite clearly across the field, and he could hardly miss the dazzling green of her companion's outfit which should tell him that she had found something to occupy her. Why did he keep calling in that disturbing way?

"Jessica."

She made no effort to turn but continued as before

staring at the happy little man seated cosily among the
bracken spines. Peter's voice disturbed him not a whit.

Peter ran and then stopped. But not for long enough to
think about what he should do. It was a natural reflex
action that made him come on again and seizing Jessica
by the shoulders swing her round, away from the hedge.

"Oh," gasped Jessica, spluttering as if she'd held her
breath for too long under water.

"Why didn't you answer?" demanded Peter crisply.
"Didn't you hear me calling?"

"Yes, but I didn't want to."

Jessica was merely stating a fact. While she had stood
watching the green man she had desired nothing in the
world to interrupt them.

They both turned to the figure in the bushes. He had
moved his head at last, was nodding and smiling in their
direction, but he did not get up and he did not speak. A
little awkwardly Peter said:

"We didn't expect you. . .in the bushes like that. . ."

The man looked out past them over the landscape as
if they were dismissed from his notice.

They made their way back to where Ann was resting in
the grass.

"What made you come after me?" asked Jessica,
shivering.

"Look around. It's all changed."

Every tree, every bush and grass blade showed quite distinctly the sad weariness of late autumn. They might have
found it a mild day if they had been more suitably dressed.

"What's happening?"

"I don't know," said Peter grimly. "We seem to be in
different seasons from one moment to the next. At least in
this one Ann's antennae work better."

Ann rose from the grass as they approached. She seemed
excited.

"We've got to keep going. It's easy now."

"Did you see — " began Jessica.

"Yes. But we've got to move."

Ann's shoes were well adapted to the tough walking she now had to do. The others scrambled after.

"Look," said Ann suddenly. "Isn't that it?"

The stretch of grassland rose to an open sky. Gulls and a sea boom drew them on, up to the flat shelf. They were farther round the southern end of the bay than even Peter had been the day before.

A figure loomed ahead from a heap of stones and stood as if awaiting their coming.

"It's Duguth," said Ann with an excited tremor in her voice. Near-sighted she might be but nothing could prevent her recognising him.

Duguth waved them over. For the only time since they had come through the bramble hedge, Ann deserted the trail and walked directly towards the cloaked figure.

"It's all right," said Duguth, noticing the others hesitate. "That way leads only to the furthest stones. There is nothing there. The barrenness would drive you back. It is enough that you have come to this sea ledge."

"You expected us?" said Peter.

"Did I not say that when you discovered the circle was around you, you would come back to me?"

Peter said deliberately: "It is not a circle, you know. Only half a one."

Duguth smiled faintly.

"I have some advantage over my people," he said, "but in many things I must remain a dullard. Even I, though, looking at the crescent moon, can see clearly the shape of the full moon patterned in the heavens."

"Yes," said Peter, "I understand that. But the moon is there all the time, and it becomes full eventually. Whereas we've come to the sea's edge."

"What of it?" asked Duguth.

Peter stared helplessly at him. Where did you go when you got to the sea? His mind went back to May of that year — to the battle of Dunkirk. When the British soldiers

58

reached the coast, they had had no way to escape the enemy. On that occasion every vessel in England had gone to the rescue.

"Push off in a boat," said Duguth gently.

Water swayed around Peter and the Captain came vividly to mind, bending over his reels without once looking up. He remembered the tentacles of land creeping round to encircle them, to prevent their exit from the bay.

The circle around you, Duguth had said.

Peter glanced quickly at the coast. The land prongs lay apart as they should. South was not yet north. Not yet —

"You need not fear," said Duguth. "The gates have not closed."

"The gates — " said Ann, unable to stop her teeth from chattering.

"Come," said Duguth abruptly. "Let us get back quickly and find something for you to put on. I will answer questions on the way. In the meantime you girls wrap yourselves in that."

He unbuckled his cloak and tossed it to Ann and Jessica who, huddled in its warmth, proceeded three-leggedly to follow Peter and their guide down the slope and round into the inner part of the bay, back to the place they had first arrived on the day they took the road from Pengaron to the sea.

8

As they went Peter kicked at stones that the weather had loosened along the cliff. They were exposed now to the stinging freshness of a full tide in the bay. Brittle grass stalks crunched under Duguth's boots. Every now and then he would give an extra stamp that interrupted their progress.

After five minutes of silent trudging Duguth spoke.

"The first question is yours, Peter."

"Why. . .how. . .has everything changed?" demanded Peter, unable in spite of himself to keep the shivering out of his voice. "It was summer when we left Pengaron, but now — "

"Now we move into winter. Your world has drawn close to Gwynod, but not close enough for our seasons to coincide."

"Then what — "

Duguth interrupted.

"The next question is Ann's."

Ann was taken by surprise as she was brooding on something.

"You said 'gates' just now."

"Yes," said Duguth, "You want to know about them?"

"Please."

"As you followed the circle round you must have found gaps."

"At the stile. . .the station. . .the road. . .two roads."

"And you know another one, Peter," said Duguth.

The boy glanced at the sea and flinched.

"I'm not sure — "

"Well," said Duguth, "suppose, each of you, that here is a settlement, mainly of farmers. Now, imagine a wall

60

ringing that settlement. Where would you place it?"

"The semi-circle," said Peter carefully, "runs from one end of Pengaron bay to the other. It arches inland almost to Duffryn, but does not take in the railway. Then it runs round behind Pengaron and cuts through two main roads: one goes south from Duffryn and one runs north between Pengaron and Porthglas."

"Well done, Peter," said Duguth. "You have plotted it well."

"We didn't cover it all," Ann felt she had to confess. "We didn't complete the north part."

"That doesn't matter now," said Duguth. "You know its limits. You are within that boundary. Now, where there is a wall, there will be gates. For a short space of time they will allow you to go out and in."

"For a short space!"

"It may be the gates will begin to close."

"We couldn't get through at the station yesterday," Ann confided, "and we couldn't cross the bridge into Duffryn."

"It is happening already then," muttered Duguth.

It seemed to the girls, bounding awkwardly behind, that he was striding faster.

"But. . .we *could* get through today."

"That may be," Duguth's voice floated back. "Have you seen a man close his eyes in sleep? The lids quiver and open every so often. When the full weight of nature is behind them they shut tight. We have no time to lose."

Further round the bay, however, he slowed and said:

"Jessica, it was not my intention to overlook you. I am practical like all my people, but there are other things beside. What question do you wish to ask?"

Jessica swallowed in a hard dry throat, aware that her diminishing breath would have to compete with the screech of gulls.

"Can you. . .tell. . .about. . .the green man?"

Duguth stopped so suddenly that the girls almost collided with him. His face, nettle-skinned where a

61

beard might have grown, loured like a tempest.

"You have seen a green man?"

"In the hedge — " Jessica tried to speak boldly but found herself burbling. "He was sitting there watching — then he disappeared and came back — only I don't know *where* he went because the trees changed and the hedge and he was just there smiling and staring. . .and. . .and. . ."

Jessica's pounding heart held up the final revelation.

". . .he was green all over."

"I know him," said Duguth calmly now. "At least I know his kind. And I can tell you it is a pity he has seen you for there is danger in the eyes of these men."

Jessica's own eyes opened very wide at this. Duguth seemed to speak jokingly but his face remained solemn.

"If you treated him to such a look, Jessica, he would have met his match. If he were a spy, as I suspect he was, he would have been spied out of countenance."

"Oh," said Jessica, remembering unhappily the way in which the stranger had held her gaze.

"I see," said Duguth sombrely. "He has already tried his influence."

Jessica made no answer for she felt that Duguth understood well enough what had happened. Peter, however, was growing restless. He wanted information.

"Why should there be danger?" he demanded. "Who is the green man and why should he be spying? What has any of this to do with us?"

Duguth said softly: "No more questions now. There are things you have to learn and some of them I must tell you. The first necessity is to find covering for you and the girls."

As they approached the centre of the bay Duguth slowed once more and addressed them.

"Peter, have you noticed any difference?"

The boy nodded.

"On this side of the bay?"

Peter had hardly raised his eyes past the immediate line of coast.

62

"Yes," he said shortly.

"I only test," said Duguth, "to see how fully you have entered our world of Gwynod. For a time it is possible the lights and shadows will overlap. That is why the seasons shifted for you."

He half turned to the girls and pointed across the bay.

"Tell me what you see."

"Caer Owen," said Jessica, quick as a bird.

"Look carefully," said Duguth. "Pretend you are walking towards it. What does Caer Owen look like with the sun this side of its shoulder?"

Jessica stared across at the dark mound. The full tide, spraying hard against the rocks, salted the view. It was Ann who worked out Duguth's meaning.

You would have to cross grass in order to actually walk to it. Then the sun on this side of its shoulder? At the moment the sun was edging the water on their left, coming up swiftly as a winter sun will, to its westward point of departure. If the sun was to be over the shoulder of Caer Owen then she had to be on the other side. Ann pictured herself moving to the place which Peter had said was only a broken ring and scattered stone. Never had she seen such a massive spread of stonework. And there was the sun glinting behind its left flank.

With the rays of light in her eyes she went doggedly forward, aware of battlements rearing ahead where before there had been a collapsed nothingness. Somewhere too there was life about it. She could hear voices and trampling of feet.

Duguth's voice called her as from a distance.

"No further, Ann. It would be dangerous to go too near. You will be noticed in the clothes you are wearing."

Ann trembled as she found herself once more beside the others in the bay.

"It is — " she said, " — it really is — a fort. . .or a castle. . .or — "

Words wouldn't do. It was much more than any of these things.

"Something like that," said Duguth with a wry twist to his mouth, while the others gazed stupidly at Ann's radiant face, then past her out to Caer Owen.

"Yes," said Jessica, for whom an outline was taking shape. "Yes, I can see it now. It's huge."

"Come," said Duguth, turning once more and preparing to stride ahead. "We are bordering on enemy territory."

This time, however, Peter did not move.

"Where *are* we going?" he demanded in a rebellious voice.

"Why," said Duguth, interrupting his walk but not neglecting to stamp a little on the ground at the same time, "where should we be going if not home to Pengaron?"

Where the road leading inland broke from the coast's stony causeway Duguth paused.

"This track," he said, "will carry us with it. The power of an ancient road is strong. Before this was laid the way was formed. Reach down beneath layers and you will find a path no wider than a man's feet. Let us use this power that has been built up by generations. Let us tread in an old desire to reach home. Stand close, Jessica, Ann. Now, see yourselves walking up into Pengaron."

The air broke around them. In a more sheltered place, beneath trees that had retained some of their autumn richness, they found themselves on the last stretch of road leading to the village. Peter stared. He could have believed he really was approaching Pengaron were it not for a group of small children, roughly clad, at the head of the lane. They were engrossed in some game that involved the tossing of pebbles.

A woman appeared behind them, recognised Duguth and waited for him to approach. She stared at his three companions as if they had come from another planet.

"Is that the way to be dressed on a day like this?" she asked of the air as much as of anyone.

"We must give them the cloaks," said Duguth. "The

ones that Annis has been making these past weeks. They will cover the girls."

"She has made them for her own youngsters," said the woman sourly. "Keith and Marran have had them promised. What are they to do for the winter?"

"Let Annis come and tell me that herself," said Duguth. "These young people have a purpose here. We have called them and it may be they will serve us in the best possible way. We must give them what care we can."

The woman pursed her lips but nodded as if acknowledging Duguth's rightness. She went to the first row of cottages calling "Annis".

"Why is she so cross?" whispered Jessica.

"Because she cares," said Duguth.

A younger woman now came towards them, pale and strained-looking. Jessica stared hard at her. She wore the same home-spun garments that the other woman, Duguth, and the children had on. A thick serge tunic covered a thinner gown stretching to the woman's booted ankles. In Duguth's case the tunic was over trousers cross-gartered with a fine cord.

"You have cloaks for these two," said Duguth, laying his hand on Ann's shoulder as she stood huddled with Jessica in his own wrapping. Annis gave the children a long lingering glance. Then she sighed, went indoors and reappeared with her arms full of woven material. Ann and Jessica slipped quickly out of Duguth's cloak and Annis, with long thin fingers like pins, knotted a smaller cloak over each of their shoulders. They could smell the new wool as the folds fell nearly to the ground.

"Good," said Duguth, "they will disguise as well as warm. It is all they need."

Annis turned, her hands relieved of their burden, and looked at Peter. He was trying not to show that he was affected by the cold.

"I have given my boys' garments to the girls. But your man shall have a woman's cloak."

They waited while Annis returned once more to her home and came back bearing a cloak as she might carry a dish, extended in both hands. This she draped carefully across Peter's shoulders and fastened in front. The boy guessed it was her own.

"It is well," said Duguth softly. "They are ours now." Then he said aloud: "Come. Gammer Merton will have food waiting for us."

Treading stately in their new robes the children followed him along the lane, passing a thicker array of cottages than Pengaron, as they had known it, had boasted. They were low and thatched, each separated from the others by a yard. Pigs and chickens, turnips and cabbages, had taken the place of flower beds.

At the beginning of the war, Peter remembered, everyone had been asked to grow vegetables. He stared. You'd think these strange people had patterned their lives in the knowledge of Hitler. Or was it simply as Duguth had said — they were a practical people?

Before they reached the end of the village they encountered a group of youngsters clad in the woven tunics and leggings that seemed common dress for children. They were dragging along branches and logs in rope slings, as if it were their special job to provide winter's fuel for the community. They stared cheekily at Peter and the girls, and pointed to the cloaks.

Jessica walked ahead with Duguth, not much caring to be pointed at. Meanwhile the sounds of village life, rolling of carts and shooing of geese, gave Peter and Ann a chance to talk.

"What's wrong, Peter?"

"Like what?"

"Like you not getting on with Duguth."

"Oh. What have I said?"

"You're always contradicting. Or interrupting. Or only half agreeing. He must see that you don't like him."

"You girls are like sheep," said Peter. "Someone's got

66

to probe into things. You let a stranger come and boss you about and never say squeak."

"It's not like that," said Ann getting hot. "You're poisonous."

Peter made no answer but stalked stonily ahead.

They came to a stop outside the only dwelling that so far appeared to have an upper storey. It was made of solid blocks of stone and the doorway was cobbled round in a manner that reminded the girls of the school house at Duffryn. Duguth led them straight in. The room was homely and timbered, with the mellow warmth of oak furniture. The floor was partly burnished, partly covered with strips of rush matting. There was little light from the narrow windows. It was the fire that gave a flickering red glow to everything.

An old, old woman, with a ladle clutched in her fist, greeted Duguth.

"I have brought our visitors," he said. "Let us have our meat, Gammer Merton, and then our talk. When the Elders are ready they will join us."

Jessica's heart sank. She guessed they were the old men from Gullzin he referred to.

Duguth made them sit down at the long board of a table, and they waited while the old woman crawled crab-like between her cooking pot and their plates. Ann and Jessica were puzzled at first by the strong-flavoured flesh, but Peter guessed that it was hare. Hunger helped and soon each of their faces was buried in the rising fumes. When they had all reddened with the heat of food and of fire, Duguth sat back and said:

"It is good that you come at this season. Any other time of year and the land would have claimed my attention. Or absence from it would have burdened my conscience."

Jessica exclaimed: "You work on the land?"

"Indeed," said Duguth. "I am no different from the rest of the Glyphs."

"Gliffs?" said Jessica puzzled.

67

"We are inhabitants of Gwynod," said Duguth. "Farmers who occupy the territory of the circle."

"But — Pengaron — "

"— is occupied by your people also. Light folds our planes of existence differently. That is all."

Jessica wasn't sure of understanding even if she gave Duguth's words her full attention. One thing she was curious about, however.

"Why do you have blue eyes when everyone else has brown?"

Duguth looked at Jessica with new attention.

"You are quick to see," he said, and laughed self-consciously, for the azure glowed deep beneath his lids and could not be hidden whatever way the man might glance.

"The Glyphs themselves rarely notice," he murmured. "But if you would know the reason, my mother was not of this people."

"Where was she from?" asked Ann.

"She belonged to a tribe called the Cenarti. They came to this country long after the Glyphs were already settled on this soil. The ground must have had a special power even in those days to attract men like the Cenarti to it. A few skirmishes they had with the other settlers before they learnt to appreciate the hard-working farmers, what they could do with the land and what they could do with cattle.

"Then they formed the strangest union you can imagine, and yet in the end the most natural. For what one lacked the other made up. The Cenarti were clever, inventive, curious. Only they were not attached to the land as the Glyphs were. They needed the others' ability to mine and build."

"What did the Ken. . . .Ken-arty invent?" asked Jessica.

"They were interested in probing the secrets of the universe and drawing on powers in nature. When enemies came (as happened often in those days) they designed

68

swords to surpass all ordinary weapons. Their warriors' cloaks alone knotted more protection than armour. Glyph and Cenarti joined as one to defend this land."

"Something happened, though," said Ann, sensing disaster.

"Foolishness was what happened," said Duguth. "When all outside enemies were beaten, Cenarti men-of-learning began to forget they had anything in common with the Glyphs who tilled the soil. They grew remote, proud, and irritable. Only one it takes to stir these things in others, and distortion grows apace. The Glyphs had their own strength and retorted. Some of the Cenarti's handiwork — wonderful treasures — were destroyed.

"The most precious of all, the Plate of Alquar, was lost to the Cenarti. It was no ordinary work either in substance or design, for the artist had striven in it to capture the magic of union between the two peoples. Its shape was a Mandala — a circle that contained a square. Perfection joined with strength."

Ann started. There was something she must try and remember.

"As the wrecking grew, the Cenarti became more and more fearful. Something, it seemed, had grown up among them — "

Duguth passed his hand over his eyes.

"This was a long time ago, before I was born, and the stories people tell do not explain everything. Many will not even speak of how Someone came into being — "

"Someone!" exclaimed Peter.

"*Someone* call it, or *Something*. A Power belonging to neither tribe, but which seemed to grow out of their dissension, sprang up and gave orders."

Peter's voice rasped from across the table.

"If people won't say, then you can't know, can you?"

Ann clutched a hand across each elbow. Duguth was halted for a moment, not immediately absorbing Peter's hostility. When he did, his words smacked harshly back.

"Your understanding is lower than the Glyphs', boy. The sky ends at your garden fence."

The children sat stiff and awkward before the man's displeasure. Peter fixed his gaze on the table, and when Duguth resumed his voice sounded strained.

"Let us say that the Cenarti and the Glyphs were both to blame. Finally the Cenarti retreated, carrying away what treasures were left and, more important, their learning, leaving the minds of the Glyphs in a half-darkness that continues to this day."

"Where did the Cenarti go?" Ann ventured to ask.

"Into the stronghold of Caer Owen."

The girl blinked in astonishment.

"You saw how it was today."

Ann remembered that she had had to strain her neck to see to the topmost battlements.

"The Power that came between us," said Duguth whose tone had returned to normal, "has the name of Magob, but for us he has no face. He is best summed up by his actions: he forged Caer Owen out of the bitterest layers of rock. It signifies the imprisonment of two peoples, one unable to depart and the other unable to reach to those within. It is governed by something mean and violent."

Again he paused and again the children hung with rapt attention on his silence.

"The Glyphs do not understand," he went on. "But why should they? Their days are only half lit since they lost contact with the Cenarti. They are content to toil and eat and obey when Magob snaps his fingers. Something smoulders in them though, half fear, half disbelief. They do not question, but they are weary, and now — "

Duguth broke off and seemed this time as if he had really reached an end.

"You told us that your mother was Cenarti," Ann prompted.

Duguth nodded. "Having Glyph and Cenarti united in my blood makes me restless. 1 fret sometimes against the

70

bounds Magob sets us. He has fixed us in his circle and we know when there is a hedge we must not pass or a thicket beyond which we must not enquire. Sometimes if we seek further than our limits the ground outside the circle is misted over. Yet trees there are I know, for in the spring I have smelt their blossom. The Glyphs swear they know nothing of these things, and I have long suspected that my Cenarti mother has given me a wider-ranging faculty."

He looked keenly at the children but they gave no sign as yet of weariness.

"I will tell you," he said, "how my father as a young man, before ever I was born, was drawn by the Boujacks into a daring escapade."

"The Boujacks?" queried Jessica.

"Magob's men who keep the fort. In those days there was a host of stories about the Cenarti dwelling in the heights of Caer Owen. Magob it seemed had promised that his men would afford them protection. They might even have imagined the Boujacks would be their natural servants. At any rate, once they had vanished inside they were never seen afterwards — except on one occasion."

"Perhaps they all died," said Peter, drawn in now in spite of himself.

"No," said Duguth. "It is my belief they still exist. My father, however, determined to find out the truth of the legend. He entered Caer Owen one day as bold as you please along with the Boujacks. It was one of their public festivals when they drank freely in front of the Glyphs. My father pretended to be as much in his cups as they were, thinking that once inside the fortress he would easily outwit them. He went with the Boujacks through to their guard room, singing as lustily as they, slithering down stairs to make them laugh, and marching round after them in a kind of mockery that they thought was a joke. Had he not regarded them as fools he would not perhaps have been such a one himself.

"He thought, since his drunkenness was a pretence, that

71

they would sleep before he did. But he was wrong. They caroused throughout the night and did not sleep. They went on duty during the day and did not sleep. They relaxed for another evening and did not sleep.

"My father nodded off and woke to find himself deposited in a bare corner of the room. His captor friends had thrown him down as they might drop chewed bones, to be cleared up with the rubbish in the course of time. He understood now that they had resources he had never before imagined.

"A moment came when he was able to creep out into the body of the castle. There he discovered what the cunning of others had concealed, a spiral set within the thickness of the outer wall.

"The stairs were dark and airless except where occasional slits deep in the outer stone afforded him an arrow of light and a smell of sea air. Opposite each was a door etched in the wall, corresponding to the different levels of the castle; first the kitchens that lay above the guard rooms; next a sombre hall that he associated instinctively with Magob himself.

"When the last slit came round the light fell on a blank wall. He searched with both hands for another spring — until the stairs narrowed to a spearhead. Above was solid roof, and the shock drew bitter tears from him. When he struck upwards in frenzied anger the stone gave way. A shaft of light came down like a sword on his head, accomplishing what all the horrors of the dark had failed to do: my father fainted."

Duguth frowned as if it were difficult to join threads in his own memory. The children waited patiently until the pull of their hard-fixed gaze drew him slowly back.

"My father lost his senses — crumpled — and came to in what he thought was another world. A tall girl filled his vision. She had blue eyes and dazzling white robes with a strange pattern flowing through their folds. Several times he heard her murmur 'Non-Cenarti'.

72

"Later he discovered that he had emerged from the ground flag of a stone fireplace, unused now it was summer-time. People flitted in and out of his gaze while he lay recovering strength. Strange people, who sometimes reminded him of sunshine and sometimes of moonlight. He could not tell whether their hair was gold or white. They were taller than the Glyphs and all their robes were bordered with strange designs. Once the room was invaded by children, laughing and sporting, though they were older than those among the Glyphs who would be earning their bread.

"As he recovered my father explored the room he was in. The walls had been hung from ceiling to floor with rich tapestries containing a great deal of gold thread. They had been woven to give the impression of a forest. As the golden patches in the tapestry caught the light they poured sunshine between the trunks. Sometimes a deer dipped antlers into a pool.

"He began to see how the Cenarti had recreated for themselves the glories of a world they had long since left. From the topmost battlements they could observe the stars and practice their ancient mysteries. But when they looked down they beheld only a distant shimmer of light they knew was the sea. They could not look out on the landward side or see anything that would remind them of their old association with the Glyphs.

"From day to day my father grew strangely weary. The Cenarti Elders were charitable but they did not consider him clever enough to converse with. Surrounded by their cool dignity he yearned to return home.

"The girl, Maia, was able to tell my father many things about Magob's power. It is from Cenarti discoveries that he draws his cunning, as it is from Glyph labour in the fields that he takes food for his people.

"My father heard of the great staircase that winds from the front portals of the castle and ends at the doors of the Cenarti realm. He noticed that those doors were barred on the inside and that it was the Cenarti who had the privilege of undoing the bolts. So sure was Magob of his mastery.

"Then Maia showed her affection for my father by promising to return with him to his own people. The dark spiral that had brought him there took them down into the bowels of the fort. They emerged on a ledge that ran round the sides of a circular cavern which must have been the general storehouse for the castle.

"A tunnel led them out to a wall face which, at a touch on a spring, gave access to the beach. The main gate to the castle is on a higher level, approached by the road. But you know already that the rock on which the fort stands goes right down to the water."

"But," said Peter, "it means that anyone can get in that way now."

"Anyone willing to make the attempt. The rock can be under water when the tide is high. My father was lucky when he opened it on this occasion."

"I suppose it wouldn't be a safe place to visit," said Ann.

"The Glyphs never attempt it."

"Is that the end of the story?"

"Not quite. There are things about that last tunnel you have yet to hear. They will concern Peter particularly. My mother used to say that Magob did not need the Boujacks to guard that entrance. There was something belonging to the tunnel itself that few men would face."

"Your mother was Maia," exclaimed Jessica. "That is why you have blue eyes."

Duguth nodded.

"My mother was a brave and clever woman who taught me many of the ancient arts of her people. It is why I have been able to call you three today."

At this point Duguth was interrupted. Gammer Merton entered and moved heavily towards the table. Behind her, in line, creaked the old men they had met on the beach, looking more like wizened crabs than ever. One of them was wheezing badly. Jessica found to her disgust that she was nudged unceremoniously to make room for them. The old men dropped into their chairs while Gammer Merton went to blaze up the fire and fetch soup.

"You have come in good time," said Duguth. "I have reached the most interesting part of what I have to tell these three. They are about to learn what is in store for them."

"Let us have the soup first," demanded one. "Or we shall be sitting here all day while your tongue clacks, Duguth."

"Hush!" said another indignantly. "You rely too much on your age. Duguth has thought long and hard and must be given some credit for all the planning he has done. If he can make this work, we must retire gracefully."

"Humph," said the first, and looked greedily at Gammer Merton bending over the cooking pot.

"The soup will come first," Duguth said, and relaxed into silence.

Jessica thought she had had more than enough of the grunting that accompanied the elders' enjoyment of their food, before Duguth finally resumed his story.

"It is hard to tell how long the Glyphs would have ignored the existence of Magob and his slow curdling of their lives. We have been for several generations like a beheaded chicken that continues to run round its yard."

"I object, Duguth. I object. . . .you are undermining

our work," said the grumpy elder who had wanted his soup.

"He must tell it his own way," said one of the others. "We have done little to put things right, for all our years."

"Speak for yourself, Gadger," said the first. "I've worked hard from being a boy. My family's not wanted."

"Venerables," said Duguth. "Have you not given this task into my hands?"

Two of the elders nodded and Duguth resumed.

"I think we might have been content to sit in the sun of a summer's evening. We would have slid gently with the world, paying our dues as we have always done and looking no further than our cabbage patches. Something might trouble us, but we would say: 'The parsley was not good this year', or 'We must not grumble at the storms when they help the crops forward'. Magob, however, sought to stretch us a little further, wanting from us increased awareness of his mastery. So he has done a thing that muffles our heartbeats with sorrow. What it is I shall show you when the light lessens.

"We come now to your presence here. When I saw you cross the beach the sun was not shining in Gwynod: yet you shimmered before me like dancing lights. I watched two of you sport as my father said the Cenarti children sported in the upper reaches of the fort. I remembered my Cenarti mother and how she has developed in me certain powers. I was able to call you once you turned your backs on Caer Owen."

"How — ?" began Peter.

"Our worlds came very close," said Duguth. "The circle also in which we are bound has grown in energy over a long period. I tapped that power and drew you, for a brief space, into Gwynod."

"You mean," said Peter, "that when we met you before, on the beach, we were already in your world?"

"You had to be. We have no power to enter yours."

"You have brought us again now," said Ann.

76

"Yes," said Duguth. "You are here because of me. But also, let me say, it was after you decided the matter for yourselves. Otherwise I would not have been able to detain you this long."

"We never — " began Peter.

He had a sudden recollection of brambles clutching him — and Ann unwilling to go on.

"How do we get back?"

"By following the task through," said Duguth. "You, Peter, will be able to return while the gates still allow in order to carry through the work we have for you. But you will go alone. Ann and Jessica will remain here until you re-enter".

"They'll be your hostages, you mean."

"They are needed to fulfil a pattern."

"I think," said Peter coldly, "that you have assumed a great deal."

Ann closed her eyes and wished the moment of conflict over. But Duguth was not disposed to be angry. Nor did he address Peter as 'boy'.

"Listen," he said, "there is a war waging in your world — "

"How d'you know?" demanded Peter, but a kindling in Duguth's eyes made him drop his own.

"How do I know, you would say, since I am bound by Magob's walls? Why, it is with you. There have been fires I can tell, for the charring is everywhere around. And terror and tears in full measure."

Jessica glanced quickly down at her clothes, expecting to see scorch marks.

"How you came to Pengaron you must tell me yourselves."

Ann told him, quietly, how they were evacuated and how — because they wished to remain together — they had come to be billeted in Pengaron.

"You see," said Duguth triumphantly, "how well it has fallen out?"

Not all of them felt so sure it was a matter they could rejoice in.

"Three of you it needed," went on Duguth. "Children at that. And three of you have come from outside — strangers to the power of the place — at the moment when disaster has drawn us close."

"Let me remind you," broke in one of the Venerables, "that we are only at the beginning. Nothing has been accomplished yet. We can expect further punishment if Magob finds out."

"I think," said Duguth, "he may already know of their arrival."

"What!" thundered another Venerable, causing Jessica to jump.

"His spies are abroad and we must expect him to miss nothing."

"But the retribution. Have you thought — "

"We must take that chance. He does not know *why* the young ones are with us. He will shadow any move we make until he finds out what we are after. Then there will be danger."

Jessica gripped Ann's arm, drawing merely a glance from Duguth.

"Of course the girls will stay together," he said. "They will be safe enough."

For a moment he grew remote from them, looking towards the window as if the signs of declining daylight troubled him.

"What is the work you want me to do?" asked Peter cautiously.

"Finding something we lost a long time ago. I told you earlier of the Plate of Alquar. Of all their treasures it was the one the Cenarti valued most. When the Glyphs brought about its destruction they ensured the final separation of the two peoples.

"There was much of course that was destroyed when the Glyphs grew angry. Their strength outran their sense,

78

and the cold disdain of the Cenarti enraged them. The Plate of Alquar, however, was a different matter. I think the Glyphs did not realise it could be broken.

"The man who took the Plate was no wrecker: simply a mischief-maker who thought to gain ransom and to tease the Cenarti. But the Plate would not be held by such a one. There was accident — collision — folly. It is always the mischief-maker who brings about the worst disaster. When the Plate split in two, the Cenarti lords howled. Even Magob must have heard for he came fast after.

"The Glyph — we call him Pamen now because it means 'one-of-disorder' — managed to snatch up half the Plate and make off. He was a true sprite, one who could run ahead of all trouble even with dyke-gates bursting behind.

"Magob, however, had set his ramparts, and now as Cenarti tore violently apart from Glyph, Magob's strength grew. Pamen saw as he ran that he was hemmed in. He skirted the wall until he came to one of the gaps. A shadow moved across it: Magob was shutting his gates. They were so close that a thin man could not pass.

"Yet not even Magob could reach to the mischief deep inside Pamen. With a last thrust he hurled the half Plate of Alquar through the slit — beyond our sight and our retrieval. They say it whistled sharp like a metal bird as it went.

"After that the Cenarti took all that was left to them into Caer Owen, and the fortress gates closed behind. We remained equally imprisoned, between the sea and Magob's walls, with Magob's men our overlords. They leave us alone in our village and our fields, but they take the profits of our labour. Our very cattle we cannot count our own."

"What happened," asked Jessica, "to the other half of the Plate?"

"The Cenarti carried it with them into Caer Owen. It was my mother who told me its full significance. Had the rift not been exceeding great between the Glyphs and Cenarti the Plate could not have broken. When it cracked it meant the end of all ties, all loyalties, all affection. The Cenarti were fearful of their own destruction at the hand of so close an enemy and fled to Magob's protection.

"Even then had the Glyphs been able to restore the half of Alquar's Plate that Pamen took, there might have been some hope. There was healing in the Plate that would have drawn the two sides together. But the Glyphs could not retrieve it and Magob's circle was complete."

"Did Magob get hold of it?" asked Peter, thinking how the Plate must have landed just outside the walls.

"Never," said Duguth. "And never could. Or his mastery would be such that he would not need to hold onto the Cenarti. I tell you I learnt much about the Plate of Alquar from my mother and I know the Cenarti were not angry for nothing at its loss."

"Why couldn't Magob just go and pick it up — or his men for him?"

"Because it entered *your* world," said Duguth. "Strife in our spheres has always drawn us close and for one second Pamen had the strangest chance of all. After that it no doubt lay until someone came and carried it out of the range of Pengaron entirely."

"How do you know?" asked Peter.

"Had it stayed where it fell we would have felt its influence, even through the barrier that separates us. Had it been carried back into Pengaron it would have drawn Magob's attention. Therefore when it was picked up it must have been taken further afield beyond the circle. Apart from that I do not know its fate. Except for one thing — you three have been near it within the last few days."

Peter and the girls gasped with astonishment.

"I told you I have the ability from my mother to perceive certain things. There is a radiance around you now — whether with one more than another I cannot tell, for you are linked. But I know that Alquar's Plate could give that influence to all who came close."

"That is what you want us to find?" exclaimed Peter.

"It is for you to seek, Peter, and for you to bring back here."

"Why not all of us," cried Jessica, "together?"

"No," said Duguth. "There will be danger in this. Besides, there is a kind of testing which must be gone through by the one who seeks."

"Then you don't need us all," said Ann.

"You girls are both necessary," said Duguth. "The square on the Plate had a human figure at each of its corners, two male and two female. I know that we must repeat that pattern. You three are chosen because you are children and stand outside our quarrel, but I will take the fourth place because of the link in my blood between Glyph and Cenarti."

"Why," asked Ann, "did you choose children?"

Duguth answered by rising and preparing to take them a further journey. They buckled on their new cloaks, feeling the prickle of coarse wool on their necks. It was half dark for the fire in the room had burnt low and the light outside was no longer strong enough to penetrate.

They left the Venerables sitting in heavy slumber.

The afternoon sky descended upon them and a colder wind had sprung up. The animals in the yards looked subdued in the fading light, awaiting the full tide of darkness. Men were around now and children were being hunted and hustled into homes as if they were breaking some special prohibition in being out of doors at this time of day. People stared curiously at Duguth's three companions.

"Come," said the man in his old peremptory manner, and strode ahead down the lane to the cottage from which Annis had emerged. The Pinchers' cottage, thought Jessica, for it was near enough to where they had been billeted.

Duguth bent under its low lintel and his three companions followed. The room was close, with a plethora of cooking utensils neatly laid out and chairs that were hard and straight. A baby girl sat quietly on the ground

81

in front of the fire and two boys were helping to heap logs.

"Cousin Annis," said Duguth to the woman clearing plates from the table, "you will not mind that I bring them here. They must see and know."

The woman who had given the cloaks turned and shook her head.

"It begins," she said in a low voice. "It is earlier every day."

"They have eaten?"

"Well."

Duguth turned to his companions.

"Annis is a widow and the daughter of my father's sister. These are her children — Keith and Marran there — and baby Gwilla. Our grandfather is one of the Venerables you have just been with."

Duguth went to the fire where baby Gwilla was sitting still as a mouse, dreaming into the flames. He caught her up in his arms.

"Time to lie down," he said. "You will rest till the dawn my pretty one."

The child hardly stirred as he carried her to a cot in the corner. Jessica noticed that she did not look sleepy for her eyes were open wide. Only her head drooped slightly on the man's shoulder.

Keith and Marran had come to a stop over their logs and were also looking dreamily into the fire. Annis moved behind one boy and with her hands gently on his shoulders pressed him down into a chair. He sat listlessly against its tall straight back.

The older woman whom they had met first and whose crossness Jessica disliked entered behind them. When she looked towards Annis and the boys there was a hurt in her eyes indescribable.

"You will keep them there?" she asked in the same tones as before.

Duguth came forward.

"Annis does as she must, Aunt," he said. "We have three

others to sleep tonight. Keith and Marran will not mind. They will be warm by the fire and we shall wrap blankets over them."

Peter stared. Surely these two lads weren't going to turn out of their beds for himself and the girls? And how long did Duguth intend to keep them in this 'world' of his? He'd had no idea of sleeping through a night here. What about the Captain and the Pinchers and his parents? He noticed that Ann was watching the two boys in peculiar fascination.

The second one moved at his mother's instigation, as if he had great weights attached to his limbs, into a corner where the easiest chair in the room stood. Again, Annis guided him to sit down, moving his legs into a comfortable position and finally pressing her lips to his forehead as if she were saying farewell to him for the night. The boy seemed all the while to be staring ahead as if deep in contemplation.

"What is the matter with them?" whispered Ann in the hushed atmosphere.

The older woman did not relax the tension of her face for an instant. Her daughter Annis continued to move gently around, fetching blankets to cover her sons. It was Duguth who came forward to answer Ann's question.

"Not sleep," he said. "Though we draw their lids over their eyes, it will not be sleep. Come and see for yourselves."

Ann and Peter crept after him, over to the boy by the hearth. Duguth drew his hand across the boy's shoulder but he did not respond. The eyes continued to look blankly into the fire. Annis came with a blanket and draped it round the chair frame, drawing the boy's head back into its folds.

"This is Keith," said Duguth. "An hour ago you would have found him running through the village, shouting because his work for the day had come to an end and he would be free after his meal. Now it is dusk and he is, as you see, called to a place we cannot reach."

"Are *all* the children affected?" asked Peter.

"Magob draws them all."

"But not us," said Ann quickly.

"No. That is why you will be of use."

"How long will this — trance thing — last?" asked Peter.

"Until the light returns."

"And only the children — ?"

"The power around is so strong that it must affect all the Glyphs in some way. Even you will feel sleepier than usual this evening. But the net is cast for the children. They are easier prey for Magob and he seeks to gain a hold of them before their wills are formed. Where he takes them we do not know. They themselves can recall nothing in the morning. I tell you, the winter is a dreaded time. As the days grow shorter they will spend longer periods in Magob's power. Their childhood passes and they must work during the time it is light. Our lives are hard, and the Glyphs are not a numerous people to be feeding Boujacks and Cenarti as well as our own folk. Still, we have struggled to give our children what little joy we could. Now they are no longer ours when Magob calls them. Do not ask me why. We live in the shadow of so many fears and have no grasp of their substance."

"That is terrible," whispered Ann.

As bad as waiting for the bombs to fall, thought Jessica, and not knowing where or when.

Duguth motioned them to the table to continue their conference.

"You will rest here this evening," he said. "It will make little difference to Keith and Marran if they do not occupy their beds for one night."

"But we're expected back," cried Jessica. "What will the Pinchers say?"

"You shouldn't ask that we stay the night," said Peter. "We have people who will worry about us."

"What do you propose?" asked Duguth calmly. "There

84

is nothing that can go ahead before the morning. If you try to leave the village before it is light Magob's attention will be caught. He will know you are strangers because you are not under his influence at this time when our children are."

"It is selfish," said Peter, "not to have regard for other people's worry."

He wondered how the Captain would take his absence. Perhaps the man would put on his long boots and tramp the countryside looking for them.

Duguth only smiled grimly.

"And will you, Peter, have regard for our worry? Seek and find the Plate of Alquar for us and it may be that the links will be forged again with the Cenarti. In face of that strength alone will Magob dwindle."

"Is it certain?" asked Ann in a quiet voice.

"Nothing is certain," responded Duguth. "It is long since the Glyphs have thought of making any retaliation against oppression. Because I am half Cenarti and because of this latest evil, I have been able to rouse them to some thought and some decision. They fear still, but our elders agreed to my calling you. The search must be carried out in your world and can be done only by one from your world."

He waited and Peter knew that an answer was being demanded from him. Twice he opened his mouth to speak, then closed it again. He found that he was looking down at the cloak Annis had clasped around him. Her own, he remembered.

"All right," he said quietly. "If it doesn't take too long."

As he glanced up he saw that Duguth was smiling after his odd fashion.

"We must often fight beside those we do not rate our friends," he said. Peter flushed hotly.

"I suppose," he muttered, "there must be some clue as to what I'm looking for."

"Only that it lies somewhere you have been these last few days."

"And outside Pengaron, remember," said Jessica.

"Outside the ring that encircles Pengaron," said Ann with greater accuracy.

"That's what I meant," said Jessica. "Outside horrid Magob's place."

Duguth froze and Annis and her mother both turned and looked at the assembly round the table.

"Don't speak like that," the man said sharply. "It is not a name to be used lightly."

Jessica was taken aback. She had supposed they all agreed that Magob was horrid.

"Nor do we think of our land as belonging to him," said Duguth. "He may rule and sway and bind but the land is ours."

"I don't see," said Peter who had been concentrating on his problem, "how I'm to find something that doesn't look the way it ought, that I've never seen before in any case, and could be lying anywhere between here and — and —"

"You will think," said Duguth, "and follow whatever idea comes to you. That is the only advice I can give. If you fulfil the first part of the quest then it may be that the Plate will draw you to it."

"What first part?" asked Peter, suspicious.

"There is something you must undergo for your own protection — a kind of testing you may call it. Its real purpose will be served after you have found the Plate for at that time you will be most in danger. Magob will know then what our search has been about and will try to prevent your return. If, however, you have first faced the Shadow you will have some guard against him."

"It doesn't sound very substantial," Peter said, determined now to let nothing surprise him. "Could you explain the Shadow?"

His coolness drew another half smile from the man.

"I told you of the tunnel that runs from Caer Owen's storehouse to the beach. It is there you will meet with the Shadow."

"Inside Caer Owen?" said Peter, feeling his heart lurch. "You mean — go back into Magob's stronghold?"

"You must be strengthened as metal is."

"But not there — "

"It is the only way. During that time of testing Magob will not be able to touch you."

"*What* is the Shadow?"

"Something you won't know until you meet it. The shape it takes will be for you alone."

"Oh," said Peter, remembering how Magob's wall had been different for him and for Ann and for Jessica.

"The Shadow," said Duguth, "will be something you will draw by fear or desire to yourself. You must remain and face whatever comes."

"Do you only know about it from your mother?"

"I have faced it myself, if that is what you mean. Once. Before I ventured to advise the Glyphs."

"Couldn't you tell us what it was like for you?"

Duguth shook his head.

"I came through," he said quietly. "It is enough. Believe me, it would be unwise to say the least for us to send you, ignorant and vulnerable as you are, on a mission against Magob without this testing."

"When will it happen?" asked Peter.

"Tomorrow, as soon as the tide allows us to approach the rock. That will be around noon, so we shall go first to the market at Caer Owen. The girls also. There should be no danger of discovery if you keep in the company of Annis or myself. Your cloaks will protect you from notice. We can slip down to the shore when the moment comes."

Ann gave an involuntary jolt. Tiredness was seeping through her like a shallow persistent sea. She wondered at the unfamiliarity of objects around.

"I *am* tired," Peter declared, yawning volubly.

"Yes," said Duguth, "there is something in this air you are not used to. It is time you all three slept. Tonight

Annis and my Aunt will take care of you. Tomorrow we shall make a start, and perhaps an end too if all goes according to plan."

Without any leavetaking Duguth muffled himself in his cloak against the night air and went away.

It was noise that woke them in the morning, great clattering gusts of it. Keith and Marran had sprung up with daybreak, and now with hungry expectation were opening doors and fetching pails and feeding chickens. Out in the yard they ducked heads into cold water and came up redcheeked and spluttering.

Ann and Jessica, tucked close in one pallet bed in a curtained part of the room had no need of a call from Annis.

"Whatever's happening?" mumbled Jessica.

"Day is happening, I think," said Ann.

Then the thought came to mind — Peter's day!

"It's so *cold*," complained Jessica.

The fire had died out and there would be no relighting of it before tea-time. It had been kept going most of the night because of Keith and Marran, and fuel must be saved during the day.

"Ann," said Jessica suddenly while they still had the muffled privacy of their blankets, "have you noticed?"

"What?"

"How like Mrs. Pincher Annis is. I could have sworn at first it was her. I don't mean *just* like. She's younger for one thing, but like enough."

Ann's voice through the blanket hair was incredulous.

"They're not a bit. You're seeing things, Jessica."

"They are," said Jessica stubborn with conviction. "And her mother's like Miss Jones. I know she's older and she doesn't talk and grin the way Miss Jones does, but she looks like her all the same. Isn't it funny how much nicer Annis is."

Ann didn't argue. It was time to get up anyway.

Within half an hour the girls, along with Peter, had endured cold air, cold water, and a solid breakfast of wheat cake and apple. Jessica bemoaned the thinness of her summer clothes.

"If only we'd known before we set out," she lamented.

There was a warmth in the cottage though, for breakfast with Keith, Marran, and Gwilla was a lively affair. Peter thought of his solitary time with the Captain and the meals they sat through in silence while the man relished his food or buried himself in his paper. This was a more normal existence, he thought, as Annis, like a mother, attended to her enlarged family. You wouldn't have guessed the possibility of Magob or Shadows or people shut up for generations in fortresses.

Then Duguth arrived.

"You are ready I see. We'll go down to the market and help Annis and my Aunt collect their shopping."

Annis smiled, her pale face lighting up wonderfully. Peter was pleased. He sensed that Keith and Marran wanted to accompany the visitors and appealed on their behalf. Duguth said:

"They are without cloaks. All who go towards Caer Owen today have been told to wear them. In that way you will not be remarked. Keith and Marran have their work to do here, and Gwilla will go to a neighbour."

Some of the radiance went from the party, and Ann felt quite guilty as she looked down at her covering. The mention of Caer Owen fell like a gigantic shadow across their spirits.

The morning, however, had a winter crispness, and as they approached the lane that led to the coast, the cluster of trees half sheltering the village from the road and acting as a wind brake was aglow and thick with berries. As on the previous day their job was to step on to the road and hold together. The journey was nothing to Peter, Ann and Jessica, but Annis said, strangely enough: "It is a long trail."

They had come now to the coastal path leading to Magob's fortress. The tide was throaty like a lion but the wind was not set to rouse its temper. There were others walking in the same direction, mostly women and children with baskets.

"The Boujacks insist on this," said Duguth. "What we grow in our own yards we may keep for ourselves. But the rest goes to them. They have a coin in which they pay us. Then they resell us our own produce. These market days are often turned into a festival by the Boujacks. You will see drinking and merry-making on both sides, though the women are rarely part of it."

How dull everyone looks, thought Jessica, surveying the throng of sober, grey-garbed Glyphs. Yet the children were bright-eyed and eager as children everywhere on a day's outing. A memory stirred in Jessica of a sunny platform with other children on a Saturday morning treat to Abertowyn. Then Jessica's mind grew hazy on the subject, and struggle as she might to retain the memory, it slipped from her.

Ann seized the opportunity to make up the quarrel of the previous day with Peter. Falling into step beside him she said timidly:

"What was it you noticed different about the coast? When we were coming round the bay and Duguth asked if something had changed?"

"Oh that," said Peter, "it was just that the breakwater wasn't there any more. Where the boats are kept — were kept — " Peter felt confusion spreading. "There weren't any of those around either."

He had obviously forgotten their tiff of the day before. Ann's returning happiness had nothing to do with boats. Her spirits could not be oppressed even by the monstrous stonework they were approaching.

The nearer they got the more of the sky Caer Owen cancelled out. The central fort loomed incredibly round. They could only see its upper reaches for a series of walls skirted the front of the keep. Neither slit nor embrasure nor moulding alleviated its blankness. If indeed the Cenarti were there they could not, as Duguth said, behold anything of their former lands or their old way of life.

A bank sloped down from the outer wall. At its foot, beside a wide, sluggish stream, was a clearing where rows upon rows of market stalls were set up. The impression was of a town taking the air, such a bustling was going on between. Today it was permissible for visitors to climb the slope and enter the castle courtyard where the Boujacks were holding a festival.

"Be sure," said Duguth coldly, "they are well in control."

There was one thing that the children were not prepared for, though they realised afterwards that they should have been. Jessica gasped loudest.

"Look Duguth. Look. There's the Green Man."

Duguth only smiled grimly.

"There are more over there," said Peter. "In fact there's a whole brigade of them."

It was true — the man in green had repeated himself several times over. Sweeping in behind came men in red and men in yellow and men in orange. But startled as they were by the brightness of the apparel, it was nothing to the shock the children experienced on looking at the men's faces.

"I can't see very well from here," said Ann apologising to herself for what she was seeing only too well.

"What are they?" asked Peter aghast.

"Those," said Duguth, "are the Boujacks."

"But I thought the Boujacks were soldiers."

"So they are, of a kind. Do you not see how they are regimented in their colours?"

Comics more like, fools, jesters, sturdy little men who went tumbling about to serve the stalls.

"They're all alike," gasped Peter.

Everywhere he turned he saw the same face. The green man whom Jessica had encountered in the field had worn a cap. Some of these Boujacks were bare-headed but each displayed an identical head with a cowlick across the brow and thick hair down the side of the cheeks. Only by their flamboyant colour could some be marked off from others.

"Magob's creatures," said Duguth scornfully. "Nature was drugged or drunk when it hiccupped these into existence."

"It's uncanny," said Peter. "What are the women like?"

Duguth looked hard at him.

"There are no women," he said. "None at any rate, have ever been known to exist."

Peter glanced again at the men. You couldn't tell there was any difference in age, either.

"You can't *not* have women," said Jessica. "Can you?"

"All creatures in nature go in pairs," said Peter authoritatively.

"In nature they do," said Duguth.

The children looked at each other. It was colder now than it should be even for late autumn.

Annis and her mother drew off into the throng of sellers and buyers.

"Keep close," Duguth ordered the children.

They followed at first as near as they could, but six people could not hope to remain together. Ann and Jessica became engrossed in the stalls.

"Look," said Ann. "Flowers."

She'd missed them in Pengaron as it now was. Pigs and hens had taken the place in Annis's yard of Mr. Pincher's rose bushes. Here, however, was a mass of pot marigolds, late roses, and hellebore, strewn together on a stall conducted by two men in green.

"Where do all the flowers come from?" she asked Duguth.

"Gardens that belonged to the Cenarti were taken over by the Boujacks. They have a purpose for them."

Meanwhile Jessica had drifted close to the stall. A woman was asking for "yellows". The man took an assortment in his close grip and tossed them onto the scales.

They're weighing them, thought Jessica. You don't sell flowers by *weight*.

Then the stalks were bent and they were crushed into the woman's basket. You don't do that to flowers, thought Jessica, feeling as if she were receiving the hurt. Ann joined her and they watched the process repeated.

"Flowers are beautiful things. . ."

"I suppose they use them in jams or stews," said Jessica. She didn't for one moment imagine the Glyphs would use rose petals as her mother did for scenting clothes. Or make pot-pourris of them to sweeten their rooms. They would have some much more practical use than that.

"They don't seem to see them as flowers," said Ann in amazement.

Peter said: "It must be odd seeing yourself repeated a hundred times over. Like looking in a lot of mirrors. Why do they wear such colours?"

"To cheer us up?" speculated Duguth.

Peter felt he might have asked why the Glyphs wore such consistently drab clothes. The brightness of the Boujacks was a mockery of the Glyphs' sobriety, just as their grins contrasted with the serious faces of the subject people. Peter decided that he didn't like the reds and greens and yellows. They were violent rather than cheerful when exploited in this way.

"Our soldiers dress not to be noticed," he said.

"The Boujacks don't mind being noticed," said Duguth. "They have nothing to fear."

"But the Glyphs could fight them," said Peter. "They look stronger."

"With ploughshares perhaps," said Duguth caustically. "I tell you, Peter, you don't yet know what strength Magob's servants possess."

He became suddenly aware of the break-up of the party. "Where are Ann and Jessica?" he asked abruptly.

Peter strained on tiptoe to peer round. Together they shifted backwards and forwards as the throng permitted.

"I *think* I saw them going up the slope."

"Then we must get to them," said Duguth imperiously. "They mustn't enter the castle."

It was already too late. Ann and Jessica had drifted with the crowd, hardly noticing until they came to the huge stone archway leading to the outer courtyard.

"We'd better go back," said Ann recoiling instantly. "I'm sure Duguth doesn't mean us to be here."

The girls struggled in vain against the thickening masses. They were swept on into the courtyard where everything was laid out for drinking, dancing, and music. The Glyphs who laboured so hard in their fields to pay the Boujacks now had their lips ready for the Boujacks' beer. It was of a particularly heady kind and in their generous serving of it the Boujacks were delightful.

Music, more percussion than anything, was added to the festivities. The Glyph children liked this and the Boujacks encouraged them to join in beating time. As for themselves, the Boujacks liked movement. Rows upon rows of them with hands joined behind backs, jogged together in a dance.

"Don't they look funny," said Jessica, giggling delightedly as the stocky men, all one height, arms linked, feet parallel, moved like a great segmented caterpillar.

Every now and then as the music swelled, the Boujacks, good fellows all, would come forward with their tankards towards the area where the Glyphs had congregated, and the Glyph menfolk, elated with the ale, would move towards them in return, beer raised aloft. It was a moment of pitch, with feeling and excitement on both sides. Once

94

Ann had observed this happen several times, however, she found it peculiarly monotonous — like the Boujacks themselves.

Jessica was intent on the dancing. She liked to see the men after their curiously repetitive fashion all jogging together. Her feet tapped to the rhythm and she gained some attention with her laughter. Coming after a day with the sober Glyphs and those dreadful gurgling old men, the Boujacks were a joy.

They had formed a galloping circle and were drawing in children. A Boujack seized Jessica's hand as he passed, inviting her to tap her feet to livelier effect. Others gathered and beat out the rhythm, spurring the dancers to greater effort. One or two children were dropped from the ring as the going became too strenuous for them.

Jessica, with each hand imprisoned, felt as if she were flying. It was like being on the painted horse at the roundabout. Ann should be nearby though she couldn't see where. There was only a whirl of brilliantly coloured little men. The dazzle became too great and she closed her eyes. Now, with every leap they took she felt as if she were bounding wildly through the air, only this time the steed was real and rather frightening.

The cloak was dragging hard at her shoulders. She had forgotten that when she stretched out her arms to take the Boujacks' hands it would part to show her mauve and white summer dress and her legs bare to the socks. The Boujacks' eyes were all around. Ann from a distance saw the danger and gasped, but from the moment that Jessica had been whisked away she could do nothing. There was no one to turn to, for the men were well into their drinking and the women concerned for their own families.

Jessica's steed was carrying her round at a tremendous pace and she had long since lost any assurance of safety. A terrible sickness was rising inside her. When she opened her eyes the whirling colours flew like fierce birds to her head. The movement of her feet was no longer

...ners. Like a puppet pulled by strings her body leaped mechanically on.

Ann felt her shoulder seized and she turned to encounter Duguth, angry-eyed.

"Oh," she wailed with relief and anguish. Duguth was quick to guess what had happened.

"As she comes round next time, Peter," he called, "break the circle."

Peter nodded and took up his position. Jessica was swinging at crescendoing speed, her eyes glazed, her hair running damp. He gave a sudden leap onto the man in front and tore at the hand gripping the girl's. Duguth seized Jessica's shoulders, forcing the Boujack on the other side to abandon his hold.

The girl flung tumultuously against Duguth's chest. They heard him say soothingly: "All right, Jessica. You're safe now. It's all right."

Ann hovered, concerned at her friend's painfully explosive breaths. When she was quieter, Duguth drew them away.

"That was foolish, Jessica," he said as the girl showed signs of recovery. "Foolish to wander and foolish to be tempted."

Jessica nodded, relieved that for once Peter was not saying anything. Her head ached terribly.

"You may have been spotted," said Duguth. "Your clothes give you away."

"How could the Boujacks *not* notice?" said Ann. "There were so many."

"It is Magob's notice I fear," returned Duguth. "Listen. I will explain something. The Boujacks are nothing in themselves. We call them Magob's spies because he has the power to look through them when he chooses. At that time he can see all that they see and hear all that they hear. But only if he has tuned in to these festivities will he know what has passed. It may be he has made no contact with any of his men here, in which case it hardly matters what the Boujacks themselves saw."

96

"You make them sound like machines," said Peter.

"They are human enough in their worst traits. Only I tell you, do not trust them in any way. They are under a cold and cunning influence. Let us go quickly now, for my cousin will be waiting."

The others were not sorry to turn their backs on the dark fortress with its impregnable roundness and chilling stone. They made their way easily this time through the gates and down the slope, meeting only stragglers coming up. Some of the stalls were being dismantled as having served their purpose now that the main flow of Glyphs had been drawn into the courtyard. Only the market further along was still busy with women.

As they reached the stream Ann caught a reflection in the still water of what lay behind them.

"Oh. .h. .h," she wailed.

The imposing tower had gone. Only eyes stared back at her, eyes imprisoned in shrunken faces. Wherever she glanced the water reflected them, thousands upon thousands. . . .caged, hopeless. . . .was this Magob's fort?

As Duguth swung her away from the stream Ann broke into sobs, with Caer Owen itself standing stonily aloof. The others peering down into the water caught only their own reflection, but Duguth understood.

"Child," he said, "you saw what you did because the stream could not lie to you. You have been granted the Power of Water."

The others stared at him.

"I understand now," said Duguth thoughtfully, "why there was a need for four. At each of the points depicted on the Plate of Alquar there was a figure with cupped hands. One held a fish and one a bird, another a miniature tree, and the fourth had a petal-like object that no doubt was tongues of flame. These signify the four elements: Water, Air, Earth, and Fire. For the quest to be carried through, the four channels of the natural world must take up their places. Each of you I have no doubt has the ability to draw for a brief moment upon one element. How the gifts will be distributed I cannot tell. It is up to you to discover them. With Ann it will assuredly be Water."

"Well," said Duguth's aunt tartly as they approached. "It has been a picnic for some of us."

"Indeed," said Duguth, "we have had so many goodies that we have been close to sickness. Have we not Jessica?"

The girl made no answer.

"If we walk to the far end," said Duguth, "we shall come to some suitable refreshment. You must be tired, Aunt."

"I am stronger than Annis here," she said. "Look to your cousin first."

They followed through the diminishing busy-ness of the market. Annis appeared pale and weary but Ann and Jessica stayed beside her, carrying her purchases. Duguth held Peter in the rear.

When they reached the far end of the market Ann turned but could glimpse nothing of her cousin and his companion. Annis called her forward.

"I can't see them anywhere," said Ann straining on tiptoe.

"They will have gone where they planned last evening," said Annis softly.

"You mean. . .to Caer Owen? But not without us!"

She had meant to give Peter the silver threepence — for luck in that terrifying fort. Now it was too late.

"My dear," said Annis, "we have a part to play also. If we are watched we must give no hint of having anything but an ordinary day's business in hand."

Ann and Jessica were forced to perform what had been a woman's lot down the ages, and hold themselves outwardly still and useful and patient.

11

Peter felt Duguth's hand on his shoulder drawing him aside, directing him to stop at stalls and observe their wares, then swinging him round towards the south of Caer Owen.

"We can walk on the beach now," said Duguth. "The tide will be clearing."

"But the others. . ." exclaimed Peter. "They won't know. . ."

"This is your part, Peter. It will be easier if you go alone."

Peter hesitated. He disliked slipping off without a word to Ann or Jessica. Hadn't he made a promise to his father? On the other hand he wished to respond to the call like a man. In any case he found he had to keep walking because Duguth hadn't stopped.

"Which way?" he asked doubtfully.

"If we stroll back to the road as if we are returning to Pengaron we can slip down to the shore without arousing suspicion. The Boujacks have never bothered much about the coastal side of the fort for they know we do not care for the sea. Besides, as I told you before, the entrance from the beach has its own protection."

Duguth led to a point from where they could scramble down. The sea was only just pulling out from the shore leaving brown skirts of sand around the bay. Still in its wake were rills, streams, and tributaries flowing toward their parent gulf.

"We should have given you boots, perhaps," said Duguth frowning.

"I can manage," said Peter.

"Take off your shoes then. You will have to wade the last bit."

The waters were still awash round the gleaming sides of Caer Owen. Peter hitched up his cloak and carried his shoes and socks, feeling carefully across the rough surface of rocks with his bare feet. Round his calves the water ran icy. They clambered where they could through the needle points at the base of the cliff, rising from the water like fins of small fish attendant upon a whale. Only once did Peter look directly upwards.

"Don't do that," said Duguth quickly.

It was too late. Peter was reeling giddily.

"We are at an angle," said Duguth, "where great physical power can shatter confidence."

It's monstrous, thought Peter, and *vibrating*. He wasn't surprised the Glyphs wouldn't come near. He recalled the pull the rock alone had had on him when he first visited it. Over those inside the fortress, he thought, its power must be much greater.

Duguth went ahead now, clambering up the first slope of cliff. This part, as far as the ledge, was easy. After that the stone grew smooth and vertical so that it was difficult to say where cliff ended and fort began. The sea had lately covered the ledge for it was dampish dark with specks of crannied weed. Peter hardly saw where his companion touched before a section of rock creaked back a few feet into space.

"The tunnel," said Duguth as Peter stared into it, "may wind but it will not branch. Go straight through into Caer Owen's cellars. There will be light when you reach the ledge circling the storehouse. Follow it round as far as you need and return to me here. Fear nothing from Magob until after the Shadow has gone. That at least he will have no jurisdiction over."

It was Duguth's old tone of command.

"Is that all?" asked Peter.

"It is enough."

No word of encouragement. No sympathy for doubt or fear.

100

It's dark, Peter thought, but it would be useless to ask for a torch or matches or anything that a mere boy scout would think of. Not in that game now, boyo, he told himself. Duguth remained still, leaving the timing to him. He's so confident, thought Peter, that everyone will jump to whatever he tells them. Well, suppose I don't?

He hesitated for so long that it seemed to him the man *must* say something. But Duguth remained in a state of repose, his shoulders lodged against the rock, leaving Peter to choose his own time for going forward.

The sea was pulling further out, stronger in the end than Caer Owen. Even that monstrous citadel could not hold the tide forever to itself, though the water swirled reluctantly round its lower reaches. For so many hours in every cycle this entrance to the rock was uncovered. Each day a chance was given to the Glyphs. Each day it was allowed to pass.

A wind blew along the ledge, striking Peter briskly on the cheeks. He gathered his cloak about him, its soft folds reminding him of Annis and her boys. Keith and Marran were confined to the village this day. They would remember it in future years as the time the visitors took their cloaks. What would they feel later about such a day? Only events now would decide.

A flight of gulls screeched long-throated as they skirred the waves. It was the last sound in Peter's ears as he stepped through into the rock's still corridor and left Duguth alone to his meditation.

He forgot almost immediately what lay behind him. The tunnel was warm and close. The gap he had come through let in some light briefly. After that his eyes grew accustomed to the dimness and he began to guess at where the tunnel bent and what the walls were like. It was wider than he had expected though the roof in places was not much higher than his head. At one point he stretched out both arms sideways and touched nothing. He carefully edged over until his hand rested against solid rock.

Duguth had been right that it would wind. It almost wiggles, thought Peter, keeping to the wall. Like a snake. The thought no sooner flitted through his head than the idea took shape. He suspected the ground of humping in the middle. He had put his shoes back on before climbing the cliff but had a ridiculous notion that if he took them off now the floor would have the most unexpected feel. Smooth, he thought, like walking on very tough skin.

As the impressions accumulated everything began to roll. Peter was pitched from one wall to another, striking his left shoulder very hard. He pulled at his cloak, feeling it grip tight around his neck. Suddenly he was being carried forward at an alarming rate. A red glow came towards him. He felt himself flung helplessly out into space.

With quick understanding Peter knew that he was in the Boujacks' cellar. Light shone like a red pool below and in front of him. The ledge on which he landed had been just wide enough to prevent a worse fall. At the same instant the cloak slipped from his shoulders and he encountered the brutal grit of rock beneath his hands and knees. Then he scrambled to his feet and he wasn't any longer in a tunnel or a cellar or a fort.

He might have been on a plain. The only thing registering distinctly was a rider and his horse moving slowly across his view. "Oh," gasped Peter, for the rider was clearly a knight and his horse had not a speck of colour from white mane to white tail, except for a golden bridle and saddle. They passed proudly, the knight with his beaver up, though Peter was not near enough to observe his features. At the same time rider and horse never seemed to increase their distance from the boy.

Suddenly Peter became aware of another boy shadowing him, smaller and slimmer than himself, running to one side. He supposed that he must be running also, though how he had begun or why, he did not know. Something like a smell of sweat and dirt came to him, and there was a prickle behind his eyes. Then Peter felt his own

102

limbs bare like the boy's and in his hand was a sling and he was running with fury and hatred towards that shining knight and his pure-white horse.

Peter jerked suddenly and put a hand to his throat. He was conscious that something was missing. From the corner of his eye he could see the other boy back at his side. A moment ago he had absurdly imagined himself to be that boy. Now as they sped together Peter thought: "Oh, stop him, stop him. They mustn't be hurt. They —"

The knight and his horse were still passing in full view, the horse stepping high and leisurely, the knight with his beaver up. Peter thought their brightness was growing. At the same time he felt the boy beside him grow in force as a shadow deepens when the sun increases its glory.

However fast Peter ran, the boy kept pace with him. To his terror he was aware of his companion closing in on him as a shadow shrinks into its owner when the sun comes overhead. When he and the boy had become one, Peter gave a great whoop. Shouting all the curses he knew, he ran furiously forward as if possessed. All he wanted was to batter that vision of man and horse, rend and desecrate it.

He raised his arm with the sling and its deadly contents. He took aim with the precision of a machine. He heard the whistle of air which grew louder and louder and roared like the seas of the world coming together, and he a mere speck on their foam. As they rushed over him he sank into nothing.

When Peter came to he was lying on the ledge that ran high above the storehouse of Caer Owen. The fever had passed. He moved his legs and they scraped on rough ground. Carefully he got to his feet, thankful that the conflict was over. He was ready to set out on the quest for —

He stopped himself from going further. Surely something had stirred when the word "quest" went through his head? Peter found that he was thinking very clearly

now. Here he was in Magob's cellar. He had already wit-
nessed Magob's power over the minds of Keith and Marran.
If there was a presence in that storehouse he must shut it
out, try thinking of other things: Ann's shoes wearing
down at heel; Jessica's hair flopping.

Another thought occurred. Hadn't he told himself that
the pull of the fort would be greatest over those inside?
How long he had already been there he had no notion. But
he was desperately anxious to hurry.

"I've got to get away," Peter said. "I'll think about it
afterwards."

He followed the ledge round until he reached the
tunnel opening. He had travelled some distance down its
slope before he was struck by the cold. His shoulder was
stiff with pain from the time he had jabbed it against the
rock. As Peter put up a hand he realised with shock that
his cloak was missing. Annis's cloak. She had fastened it
on him with her own hands to be his protection.

Somehow it mattered terribly that Annis's cloak should
not be left behind in Magob's fort. Who knew what power
that might give the enemy over a family he wanted no
harm to come to? He would have to go back and search.

A small voice inside him said petulantly: "You've come
too far. It wasn't your fault."

But Peter had gained a new kind of strength. He wasn't
going to listen to the worst in him. He turned and re-
traced his steps towards the Boujacks' cellar.

When he came to the ledge he searched a long way past
the place where he must have fallen. The cloak was not
there. He approached the rim and peered over. The cellar
was full of crates and barrels. On top of one he thought he
could make out a dark bundle. That was the cloak, he
told himself, well and truly in Magob's territory.

He looked round to see if there were any means of
descent. The vault was conveniently deserted but there
was no way down. Peter crouched on the shelf and pon-
dered the problem. Suppose he jumped? That would

be the stupidest thing. The top of the nearest barrel must be twelve feet away. Besides, he couldn't get back.

What I want, thought Peter, is a hook and some rope. The strangest thought flashed through his head. Two days before he would have called it absurd. Now his situation was one of greater absurdity. He knew that this was a power-house of a special kind. The thing was, could he tap it for his own ends?

He remembered how the snake had taken shape in the tunnel as soon as he thought of it. Peter closed his eyes and concentrated. Softly he imagined it drawing towards him. When the air in front moved he did not look but thought of the drop between the ledge and the cellar floor. Something was sliding slowly down and rearing back at Peter's bidding to the shelf.

The boy held firmly in his mind's eye the picture of a spiral stair. He reached out a hand and grasped one of its rungs. Slowly, very slowly, he began to descend.

"Seven, eight, nine — " he heard himself count. Never before had he done anything so carefully. For a brief moment his mind slipped into a remembrance of a serpent and a kind of soft horror ran through his fingers and into the pit of his stomach. The rungs went from beneath his feet and something swayed, perilously.

"Stairs," commanded Peter. "Iron stairs. Open. Spiralling. Gaps between them. Fretwork — "

He was all right now. Everything returned solidly to his picture of it. As he touched the ground he turned his back on the spiral and opened his eyes. He was in the Boujacks' cellar among barrels and barrels. The harsh redness angered his sight and he looked quickly round for the cloak.

That must be it over there. He crept forward, weaving between rows of what he assumed was the Boujacks' heady liquor. Seizing the cloak, he straightaway put it round his shoulders, took a deep breath, and prepared for the journey back.

Duguth decided something was wrong. An hour passed while he watched the tide retreat. He had told Peter that no two people's experience of the Shadow would be the same. But it had not occurred to him that the time element could differ so much.

Two hours went by and the beach was wide and open. Duguth's eyes were fixed on the ebbing water, but his mind was elsewhere. Something must have happened to the boy, something engineered by Magob. Until the Shadow had passed Magob could not interfere. But what about afterwards? All Peter had to do was return along the tunnel. The Boujacks were not likely to be around that part of Caer Owen. Only if Peter had actually gone down into the storehouse itself would he be in any danger. And what would tempt him to do that?

The thoughts crossed and wove in Duguth's mind. Magob had not interfered with *him* when he had entered the tunnel and gone to meet — Duguth put away the thought of that encounter and concentrated on what was at issue now. Was there some reason why Peter should not have the same freedom to face the trials of the place and come safely back?

Of course there was. Duguth jerked as the answer came to him. He had counted on Magob allowing Peter to fulfil the quest in order to find out what the Glyphs sought. But Magob had special reason to be curious about a strange boy who entered his territory on the day before a full moon, a time when natural forces had peculiar strength. Perhaps he had decided after all to probe a little beforehand.

Duguth raged inwardly at the thought. He should have given the boy more instruction, more warning. Above all he should have told him not to pause once the testing was over, no, not for anything put in his way.

The man forced himself to be calm. Only one thing was sure — he could not enter the tunnel and search for Peter himself. Trial by the Shadow had its conditions: one who had come through could give no aid, no company, to one on the journey. Yet there were others who might help if they would.

Duguth waited until the third hour came and went. The sea was a thin band on the horizon. Then the man straightened up, shaking his cloak free of the clinging rock.

He debated whether he should leave the tunnel entrance open. If Peter returned whilst he was gone he must be able to escape. Duguth decided to leave it as it was. He would be back before the tide came again, and in any case the Venerables would be watching from Gullzin.

He turned to lower himself down from the shelf. Time was now of the utmost consequence. He strode swiftly and purposefully across the bay to where a huge idiosyncratic rock, more wrinkled than the old men who inhabited it, had the courage to front Magob's mound.

Shallow rills had divided the landscape into long islands and a mild sun bestowed a calm and a cheer that Duguth was far from feeling.

A word with the watchers. No time for more — not even to wait for the petulant sounds that meant "We told you so" — before Duguth was once more on the homeward path to Pengaron.

Jessica had been considering for the last half hour how strange it was that Annis should resemble Mrs. Pincher, yet at the same time be much younger and more "lit up" from the inside. Then the longer she studied Annis's mother the more struck she was with that indefinable resemblance to Miss Jones. Not that Annis's mother chattered or smile-flashed as Miss Jones did, but she looked and demanded in the same way. Whereas Jessica had found Mrs. Pincher sour and Miss Jones "jolly", she was inclined to reverse the distinction in this case. It was beginning to occur to her that Mrs. Pincher might have been different if her children had lived.

"It might be this influence from the past that worries Pengaron now," Ann said. "Magob's threat to the children carried on in time."

It was like the Romans ploughing salt into the land of Gaul so that nothing could grow for future generations. Jessica's eyes went very wide.

"We're not in the *past*, are we?" she exclaimed.

"I'm only guessing," said Ann. "Their clothes are sort of — "

She was interrupted by the arrival of Duguth without Peter.

Annis's mother started up saying: "What a time it's been. We came home ages — " Then she broke off and said: "Where's the boy?"

"Where indeed?" said Duguth. "He is taking his time. Let me talk to these two, Aunt. They have a claim on my news."

He drew Ann and Jessica aside and they noticed how easily Annis's mother yielded to his authority. Then Duguth told them, briefly but hiding nothing, of his concern for Peter.

"I would have waited all night and every night for his return. But tomorrow is the time of the full moon and Magob will not risk the danger of that force working against him. He will strengthen his own circle first. His gates are closing already. When they are fully shut it will be too late to accomplish the quest."

The curse of the children sown into the ground, thought Ann, for future generations always to pick up.

"It concerns you," said Duguth.

Ann responded immediately.

"You want us to go after Peter. We couldn't let him stay in that place alone."

108

"Caer Owen?" said Jessica startled.

"Why not?"

"Well done," said Duguth softly, and Ann would have gone in search of Peter ten times over to have such praise from him.

"I won't be left behind," said Jessica quickly.

"We'll keep together," said Ann.

"You may enter Caer Owen together," Duguth told them, "but you will meet the Shadow in separate ways."

He was beginning to feel doubtful now about involving the girls. His mother had come through Caer Owen but his mother was Cenarti, with all the knowledge and command of mysteries which that implied. Yet who knew what part each of them would have to play before the end? The Plate of Alquar stipulated four, and already Ann had shown she was gifted with one great Power of Nature. Of the other girl he was not so sure. She was more sprightly and might run better than the little owl, but would she stay the course?

"Is it a kind of ghost?" asked Jessica, for whom the word Shadow was already taking fearful forms.

Duguth did not answer. He had more pressing things to think about.

Within the hour they were approaching Caer Owen. A breeze had risen and Jessica's long hair which she had tied loosely with a ribbon was being lashed across her shoulders. She could hear her mother saying on another occasion at the seaside long before the dreadful war started:

"Darling, your hair will lose all its shine in this wind: come here and let me brush it."

Jessica was beginning to feel that she hadn't had her hair brushed by her mother for such a long time that it might never happen again. Perhaps she'd be old when the war ended.

"We'll have to climb," said Duguth, and scrambled ahead of them up the easier slope of cliff.

Jessica picked her way nimbly but Ann was plainly nervous.

"Here," said Duguth, returning when he saw her confused over footholds. "It's not all that difficult. You can make it all right."

Jessica went ahead to the shelf and peered disdainfully into the open tunnel.

"Don't go without me," called Ann.

"I wouldn't," said Jessica. "I don't want to go at all."

Impulsively Ann brought out the silver coin from her handkerchief and handed it to her friend.

"Here," she said. "You take this. For luck. It *is* special, you know."

Duguth had instructed them on the way, though Jessica was too wound up with nervous excitement to catch more than odd phrases.

"You understand, do you?" said Duguth finally. "Either find Peter, or else — someone must follow through the quest in his place."

"We'll stay together," said Jessica.

"Well then," said Duguth, anxious that there should be no more delay.

Together the girls went forward into Caer Owen.

"Isn't it creepy," said Jessica. "What's that?"

Ann preferred to be quiet. It was easier that way to prevent fears taking over.

"There wouldn't be rats would there?" asked Jessica. "We might as well close our eyes for all we're seeing. Pity we didn't take torches when we set out on that picnic."

It reminded Ann fleetingly of the Pinchers. They must be worried. . .

"Silly Peter," went on Jessica fretfully, "landing us in it like this."

"He came alone in the dark," Ann reminded her reproachfully.

"So he did. Supposing we call. He might hear us."

110

"You try."

Jessica found that she couldn't. The dark pulsed over her mouth and nostrils.

"Ann," she anxiously forced her lips to move.

"I'm here."

She could have sworn Ann sounded further away.

"Let me hold on to you."

Jessica stretched out a hand, but drew it sharply back again. Suppose it touched something that wasn't Ann? She came to a full stop, trembling all over. She knew she should have hung on to Ann earlier. If Duguth hadn't been watching when they entered the tunnel. . . .

"Ann," she whispered hoarsely.

This time she wasn't sure whether Ann answered or not.

Jessica's fear was growing solid around her. All the ominous words Duguth had spoken concerning the Shadow came swarming to her. She knew it would be a ghostly thing, for the ghostly thing was always lurking — in cupboards and wardrobes and round corners on stairs and in darkened rooms.

Jessica could bear it no longer. She gave a stifled bleat and turned in the direction she had come. Duguth received her as he had done once before, flung from the Boujacks' galloping ring. He caught her before she could go headlong over the rock.

She hasn't faced it, he told himself. This one is out of the running.

"Did Ann go on?" he asked when Jessica had calmed down.

"I don't know," said Jessica thinking for the first time about Ann left on her own in the tunnel.

"She must have done," said Duguth. "She *must* go on."

Jessica's sobs were mingled with a tiny, nagging sense of shame.

Ann had been feeling her way carefully along the wall. Like Peter she was better for having something to cling to.

It came to her gradually that she was alone. Jessica was going to call Peter but she must have changed her mind for nothing came but silence. Then there was a scuffling, after which Ann realised that Jessica neither breathed nor walked beside her. Duguth's words came into her head: go on whatever happens. She continued to grope her way forward.

There were still doubts, though. Perhaps Jessica had fainted with exhaustion or fright. Shouldn't she stop to find out? "Go on," said Duguth. So Ann went on.

The darkness was growing peculiarly red. She moved steadily now as the tunnel led out into a spacious vault. There was a strong smell of wood and sacking and casked ale.

She could see that she was at a level above the ground, though she had no idea how far up. Knowing she had no head for heights she avoided going too near the edge. Duguth had said: "If nothing occurs in the tunnel, follow the shelf round until you come full circle."

Well, nothing dreadful had happened so far. Ann went ploddingly, her hand pressed against the rock. After a while she had a sensation of light coming up close on the other side. She gauged from the corner of her eye that the shelf was getting narrower.

"Please God, no," she said inwardly.

For a moment she halted and turned her face more resolutely towards the wall. Then she went on. The ledge was dwindling to a mere cat-walk, and Ann knew she needed more than this. She needed enough room to make her feel confident. Already her feet were sprawling wide and her knees sinking.

She leant against the wall imagining her body was all the time swaying to the edge. If only there were a railing. Not all that open space and a great drop with it.

A shoulder against the wall was not enough. She must turn slowly and fix her back to it. She was gazing through a red haze out into fearful space, no longer able to tell where the platform's edge came in relation to her feet.

Then she allowed herself to slide down until she was sitting on the shelf with her knees drawn up tight to her chin. Finally she closed her eyes.

Somewhere she thought she heard the scuffle of rats. Sounds of all kinds came to her. Creaks and jars and a sudden scream. It was so startling that Ann opened her eyes. Everything returned to what it had been. The ledge, the light, the breathless stillness. . .

Ann closed her eyes again and waited. Gradually the noises recommenced. There were moans this time and cries of deep distress, as if the room contained people. Ann could bear it no longer: she just had to look.

The sounds went as she returned to her razor-edge state high up in the storehouse. This time, however, someone was coming towards her. A girl was tripping as nonchalantly along the narrow ledge as if she were out in a field bounded by hills. The girl stopped when she reached Ann and laughed. She turned to face the drop into space, held her arms high in the air so that her body was extended straight and fearless, and with one leap went over the side. Ann felt her own heart rise, then thud like a boulder.

Another minute and the girl had leapt back onto the ledge as if from some springboard beneath. She turned and repeated the process, bright as a button, laughing at the other's silent terror. Finally she beckoned to Ann to stand up and join her. If only she dared! Hadn't she always been hampered by short-sightedness and physical dread?

The girl went back and forth, leaping and laughing. When Ann sought to shut her out from her sight, the wailing and cries flooded back. Now the girl leaped so close that she might have been Ann's shadow. She reached out her hand and drew the other to her feet. Ann pressed hard to the wall as if her spine had grown into it.

The girl raised her arms, tempting her companion to follow suit. Ann felt her own arms go clumsily above her head. She had to forget about the drop and think only

113

that she was going to soar — as the other did — wonderfully, easily, with winged grace.

Forgetfully, Ann shut her eyes to leap. In a flash a voice from a long time ago called warningly: "Hold on." Then the room filled with shouting: anger and pain and the sound of an army marching, marching. Neither grace, nor beauty, nor wings.

"I've. . .got to. . .hold. . .on," Ann told herself, and sank determinedly down again onto the ledge. This time the sounds died out of their own accord.

When she opened her eyes she was alone. How long she had sat there she wasn't sure. But a feeling of relief told her that the Shadow had passed.

Unexpectedly the platform seemed not as narrow as she had imagined. Perhaps she could crawl where she couldn't stand. She rolled into a crouching position and began to move bellywise like a beetle. As the platform widened she had courage to stretch up. The cellar beneath was the same, angled differently. One glance into the storehouse, however, made her take a deep breath. Had she followed her shadowy companion she would certainly have suffered for it.

"I'm all right," she kept repeating to herself. "I'm through. It's over."

She had to return quickly to Duguth. A thought of the quest crossed her mind.

Ann stopped, just as Peter had done. There was something in this place which she couldn't see, a kind of presence. She remembered Peter and how that part of her mission was not accomplished. Another instinct, however, was telling her to keep going.

"Don't dither," she told herself crossly. "You're not round yet."

She edged on, sensing all the time that she was being spied on. Nothing stirred down below but in her head something was nagging.

"You're on a quest," it said, taking up her own

114

word, "a quest. . .a quest. . .a quest. . ."

"It should be Peter she heard herself retort inwardly. "I wouldn't mind going too, but it should be him really."

"A quest to where. . . ?" the thing was pressing.

"I don't know," she said in all honesty. "I wouldn't know where to begin. It should be Peter."

"A quest for what. . . ?"

"I — I — haven't seen it."

Ann was feeling bemused and her legs were very very tired. Would this nagging continue until she reached the tunnel? Somehow she was sure she'd be safe there. If only she could get out of this storehouse.

"Imagine it, then," something said.

Quick as a flash Ann answered by thinking about Maia. She didn't know why she should recall Duguth's mother, except that she must be treading the same path that Maia and Duguth's father had taken so many years before. The stairs had brought them out onto this platform and they had traced it round until they too came to the tunnel.

Ann concentrated on what Duguth's mother must have looked like — a tall elegant Cenarti fluttering in patterned robes.

". . .imagine it. . .imagine it. . ."

Ann shut out the whispers and went back to Maia. Her mind was beginning to stray to the treasures the Cenarti hung on their walls. She thought of Maia standing in front of something —

"Imagine it. . ."

Ann almost shrieked. The wall gave way suddenly beneath her hand. She had a quick glimpse of steps, the imprisoned spiral that Maia and Duguth's father had used to escape from the upper reaches of Caer Owen. Then she was through the gap, out of the storehouse of a thousand whispers, and grasping in the darkness at stone stairs which legend said would lead to the realm of the Cenarti.

13

As soon as Peter had fastened his cloak in place he felt satisfied. Annis should have no cause to think he did not value her gift. Not that she would reproach him in any way if he returned without it — Peter knew that. But her eyes would retain their sadness.

He had now only to return the way he had come — then hurry along the tunnel to where Duguth would be waiting and wondering. A sudden noise made him duck behind some crates. There was a door creaking open, then the sound of feet, half trooping, half stomping.

Another noise behind him like a hiss and a rush of air told him that his one means of escape had withdrawn. He was trapped in the bowels of Caer Owen.

Someone was rolling barrels. The festivities in the courtyard must be going better than expected for the Boujacks had come for new supplies. Magob's men, together with the Glyphs, must be continuing until late in the afternoon their beer-chanting and ring-o'-roses jollity.

The men, he could tell, were in a lusty state. Not drunk, but pleasure-heightened. He crept round to see what he could observe of them. The red light suffused their garish clothes so that from head to foot they looked as if they had had wine poured over them.

Behind them the strong portal door of the cellar stood slightly ajar. Peter contemplated dashing through — the prospect of getting out of this prison made him forget there would be dangers in the rest of the castle. But the men's business was transporting their casks through that door and at no time was it unobserved.

Then out of nowhere a hand gripped his shoulder. It shocked him more because his arm was still painful from

116

its bruising in the tunnel. A quick jump on his part sent a crate creaking. A Boujack's voice exclaimed: "A boy!"

The others swarmed at the sound. Peter got dizzily to his feet, aware that he must seem to have been spying. The Boujacks goggled with identical eyes and several exclaimed in exactly the same tones: "A boy!"

Then one said: "A big boy, though."

"In his mother's cloak," said another, and they laughed.

Peter blushed and remembered noticing that Annis's cloak fastened differently from the two boys' cloaks she had given Ann and Jessica. Theirs were hooked at the shoulder, leaving the right arm free. His was pinned at the neck centre, allowing the folds to fall evenly on either side. It was the woman's way of wearing a cloak. Peter wondered if Annis had deliberately sought to give him this protection, for the Boujacks took it he was no warrior.

"What is the boy doing here?" asked one, as if Peter were not a person to be addressed directly. They waited with a fixed jolliness on their faces.

"I — I just slipped in," said Peter lamely.

"What does the boy want?"

"To see the castle," said Peter innocently.

"Why should the boy want to see the castle?"

"It looked interesting," said Peter, "that's all."

He tried to sound like a curious child who had strayed too far. It wasn't easy for he felt in some ways the men around him, shoving each other now to get a nearer view, were more children than he was. Except that, close to, their eyes were extremely watchful.

"The best way to see the castle is in our company. We must take the boy with us."

They kept Peter in their ranks while they collected the stores they needed. Then they went together through the heavy door which the last one locked; then labouring with their burdens up stone steps and round corners and up more steps.

Peter had a vision of Duguth waiting. It occurred to him

117

for the first time that it had been no part of his mission to fall into the hands of the Boujacks, and that in doing so he might be accounted to have failed. Duguth would say he had failed.

"Blast it," thought Peter, angry with himself. "Damn and blast it!"

They reached the floor of the castle that seemed to be the Boujacks' own province, for it was a riot of reds and greens and yellows. There was, however, a series of guard rooms where the colours separated out.

Peter understood very quickly the necessity for this for within a few minutes he picked up the quarrelsomeness that existed between the "teams". Yet they're all alike, he thought, except for the colour of their clothes. As he looked around stupefied, the repetition of faces, of bodies, and of grins, made him declare inwardly: "It's crazy."

He could see now in the better light that his own captors were all yellows. He felt that in Annis's dun-coloured cloak he must be quite outstanding. Certainly the brightness of the Boujacks had begun to affect him, as if the colours contained something searing to the sight.

The men went on looking jolly even while putting Peter under escort. They led him first through their guard rooms which bordered the courtyard. The window slits were too high for Peter to see through but he could hear music and rioting still going on. It was tantalising to feel how close to freedom he was. As the Boujacks prepared to lead him deeper into the body of the castle, Peter's heart sank.

He was struck by the uncomfortable aspect of the fort. Given that a castle would have an unfailing stoniness about it, nothing seemed to have been thought of to alleviate the hard cold. The guard room was a table-bench affair. The other rooms provided neither curtains, tapestries, cushions, nor sofas. The men had not a picture nor a book nor a pin-up as far as Peter could see. A rough kind of rush matting appeared occasionally in the cells where Peter saw them relaxing over some kind of game they played with dice and counters and which they called Abax, but for the most part he could feel the chill stone strike up even through the soles of his shoes.

The archways and steps and corridors seemed to the boy to go on forever. When he asked the Boujacks where they slept, they merely grinned a little harder and showed him more of their beer and Abax. It's not a human existence, thought Peter, and remembered all the things his mother was surrounded with — the shopping, the cooking, the washing. Oh yes, said his captors, and led him up steps to a higher level of the fort where Boujacks in bands were employed over huge cauldrons and ovens and where the washing was a continuous process. Everything was very carefully regimented, but as Duguth had hinted, without a female in sight.

"What do you do when you go on leave?" asked Peter. "Do you go home?" But the men either did not understand or would not answer.

One of the things Peter discovered was that the Boujacks were untirable and unstoppable. He had long since grown weary of their journey round and through this cold and uninteresting mass of stone. But the Boujacks had begun a process they did not intend bringing to an end. Peter even suspected that the passages they took him down were ones he had visited three or four times already. Then suddenly they came into a part of the castle Peter had definitely not seen before.

An open hallway with massive fireplaces and some remnants of ornate sculpture and moulding was fronted by tall doors. Its centrepiece, however, was the most richly sculpted staircase Peter had ever seen. Only a dim light burnt here, and there was an airlessness that suggested the great doors had been barred for generations.

Peter guessed they were at the main entrance to the fort. He remembered that there were imposing doors which none of the Glyphs invited into the castle precincts had gone near. No Boujacks even went in or out; they used side entrances near the guard rooms.

Peter wondered if the last occasion when those heavy doors had been thrown open was when the Cenarti retreated into Caer Owen. He remembered Duguth mentioning a proud entry. He could picture men, women, and children sweeping up that wide staircase.

"Where does it lead?" he asked, pointing to the stairs.

The Boujacks shook their heads.

"Not there," they said. "We do not take the boy that way."

Peter guessed that not only was it out of bounds for him but it was out of bounds for them also. The men led him straight across what he could perceive in the dim light was mosaic paving and along further corridors that repeated, like themselves, the monotony of what had gone before.

There were Boujack workshops in this part, where work of the oddest kind was going forward. In one room plants were having their names punctured on leaves and stems. The Boujacks grinned at him and then at their handiwork.

Had they grown them, Peter wondered, surprised at this sign of creative activity on the Boujacks' part. Then he remembered that the Cenarti had been interested in exotic plants. He tingled unexpectedly at the thought of his nearness to the lost people.

He was urged into a further room where flowers, sorted into piles, were having their stems stamped authoritatively. *Marigold. Chrysanthemum. Rose.* It's silly, he thought. Thousands and thousands of chrysanthemums all having *chrysanthemum* stamped on their stems as if anyone couldn't recognise what they were. Besides, you didn't do that with flowers. It violated everything they stood for.

"Ouch," thought Peter, as he saw the Boujack, like a machine, sort one after another through his puncher.

"What happens to them now?" he forced himself to ask.

The Boujack grinned.

"We sell," he said. "You Glyphs will buy — sometimes."

120

"What is the boy's name?" shot a voice out of the blue.

"Peter," he answered without thinking.

"Peter," said several after him, in the same way they had each exclaimed "A boy!" Something whispered in his head that he shouldn't have told them.

They nudged him on and as they did so the boy felt terribly angry. He was tired of their eternal grins and their trivial employment. He was not in a position that gave him either pleasure or cause for merriment. He was sick of appearing interested in these routine parts of the castle. They wouldn't let him see what he wanted. He had become a plaything to amuse them, like their Abax. All the time Annis's cloak was pulling against this, reminding him of lost dignity.

He would have come to a full stop except that they jostled him on, evidently eager for what was coming next.

Peter could not have said afterwards what kind of a room he was taken into, only that there were jars which seemed to have butterflies and spiders and other kinds of small creatures stored in them. Then two Boujacks took him by the shoulders and began loosening his cloak. Peter struggled but to his astonishment it was like fighting against iron. The Boujacks looked as pleasantly back at him as if they were giving him cake and ginger ale.

Peter knew that beneath the cloak they would come to his pullover and shirt and that those garments would give him away as not being one of the Glyphs. The Boujacks, however, seemed not the slightest bit interested in his odd apparel. They slit his sleeve along the left shoulder before he could realise what they were doing, and in another second some searing instrument had been applied to his skin.

Peter shrieked. He couldn't help himself, it came so unexpectedly. It was his painful shoulder to begin with, but what had stabbed it was like a lot of red hot rods. The Boujacks continued to smile as they released him, gasping, tears bursting in his eyes. Then they laughed and pointed and Peter struggled to look sideways. Imprinted deep and clear in his flesh was *his own name*.

It was like branding cattle. Peter shouted inwardly but no sound escaped his lips.

The Boujacks gave not one sign that they understood his suffering. They were in the same merry mood that they had been all along. Peter's indignity was another form of enjoyment like their beer and Abax.

He sat on a bench, trying agonisingly to pull his shirt over the branded shoulder. He was aware indistinctly of other Boujacks coming into the room. Someone gave an instruction.

Peter had never worked out in his dealings with the men how they distinguished between those in charge and those who simply carried out commands. That there was some kind of organisation was evident, but nothing differentiated the officers' clothes from those of the others. And since they were all alike facially and bodily Peter couldn't tell how the men made their distinctions. Some device they must have, however, for he could hear a Boujack's voice saying:

"The boy is to leave the castle. It is ordered."

They were words to gain Peter's attention over and above his present agony.

The commanding Boujack came and opened Peter's sleeve, glanced at the smarting shoulder and nodded approval. Then he instructed the others briefly. Two of them made to take Peter by the arms to raise him from the bench but he started away and snatched hastily at his cloak. He knew he must be listing for the pain weighed like a ton on his left side.

They did not conduct him back exactly the way they had come for Peter had no further glimpse of the central stairway. Since the fortress was round, he guessed they probably continued in the direction they had been going before. When they reached the area of the guard rooms they led him out into the courtyard.

Peter gasped, partly at the unexpected pleasure of the air, and partly because everything was silent and in darkness. He had had no idea of the passing of time within the castle, but it seemed that more than half a day must have gone by. The revellers in the courtyard would have gone home long since.

Flares staggered the darkness all the way to the portcullised gates. Peter thought he caught a reflection from the stream at a distance, then he was out on the incline with the fort closed against him.

He stood alone and peered into the windy dark. The countryside held its eternal primitive mystery at this moment when the sun was furthest removed from it. Peter staggered down the slope no longer having to pretend to any kind of bravery. There was a coastal path he had to take to reach the road leading to Pengaron. Duguth would no longer be waiting on the shore.

He was glad now above all things for Annis's cloak. When his shoulder screamed, the cloak lent it comfort. When the wind attacked, the cloak was shield and bulwark.

He felt his hearing sharpen as it had done every night since he had left his own home. The sea sounded alarmingly close in the dark and he wanted to run down the slope on the path's other side to get away from it. The earth would be soft and the trees would be something to cling to. He knew, however, that once off the road he would stand every chance of losing his way.

He tried instead to listen as he went. He recalled the owls whose hoots had made long channels in the dark when he was lying awake in the Captain's cottage. He would have welcomed them now as a familiar thing. The noise of the sea so close at hand, so huge and powerful in the enveloping night, excited more fear in him than the whole of Magob's fort had done.

Yet by the time he reached the road branching off to Pengaron the sky had lightened. Objects were clearly discernible. There *was* the sound of a bird, only not an owl.

Cocks don't crow in the evening, Peter thought, hardly understanding why the sky ahead was trickling into brightness.

Before he reached Pengaron it came to him. Much more than half a day had passed since he left Duguth contemplating the retreating tide. Almost a whole night had followed that day, though he was unaware of it in Caer Owen for there had been no sign that the Boujacks ever slept. His own tiredness he had put down to the exhaustion of events.

It was the dawn of a new day that Peter had come to, and even the dawn had gone by as he stumbled into Pengaron.

Jessica knew as soon as she awoke that it was still night. The curtain shielding her bed had been lifted and she could glimpse embers glowing in the grate.

Strangely enough she had slept well since her adventures of the day. Duguth had seen to it that she had exercise and plenty of sea air. He had sent her running along the beach with a message to the watchers on Gullzin while he went on waiting for Ann to emerge from the tunnel.

Only Ann did not emerge. When the tide turned and the afternoon grew misty, Duguth had taken Jessica back to Pengaron. Weary and seablown, she had slept for hours. She woke in the evening and nibbled at oakcake because there wasn't much else to do. Annis's mother looked at her as if she would have liked to say a great deal, but Annis's quiet presence restrained her.

Then Jessica, in the warmth of the cottage, dropped back once more into sleep. It was Duguth's voice that woke her now. She opened her eyes to see him standing at the foot of her bed along with Annis and her mother. The three faces together gazing solemnly down at her made Jessica start.

"Jessica," Duguth was calling.

"What is it? Is Ann back?"

"No."

"Peter — "

"They are neither of them returned," said Duguth. "You must prepare yourself."

Jessica shrank down into the bed. To the girl's view the three faces had joined into something menacing.

"We must send you," said Duguth, "to find the Plate of Alquar."

Jessica gazed dumbfounded at him. The faces hung bodiless over her in the sombre light.

"Make yourself ready. There will be breakfast prepared for you. Then I will set you on the path as far as I can."

Annis moved round the bed to help Jessica and the girl tremblingly followed through all the preparation that was needed.

"She is well rested," observed Annis's mother, a remark for which Jessica hated her.

"It's still dark," she heard herself whispering.

"It will be dawn soon," said Annis. "You cannot leave the cottage until first light, and by then Keith and Marran will be stirring."

Jessica wondered why on earth it should matter to her whether Keith and Marran were stirring. Or whether they had a day's work ahead of them. It annoyed her that Annis's thoughts were taken up by her own family.

When Jessica had put on her clothes and scrubbed her face, Annis gave her breakfast. Duguth came and sat beside her. His expression was more determined than ever.

"Listen well, Jessica. There will be no time for me to

repeat these things. It was to Peter that we assigned the job of finding and bringing back the Plate of Alquar. Peter would have been resourceful and strong. Had Ann returned after coming through the test of the Shadow it might have been possible to send her in his place. They have both failed to emerge from Caer Owen and the rock has had to be closed against the tide. So — "

Ann locked in that fort! Jessica felt all the safe things in life crumbling.

"So," he said, "we shall have to send you because you are all that is left to us."

"I can't," wailed Jessica. "I wouldn't know where to look."

"The Plate of Alquar rests somewhere in your world. You have been near it at some point during the past week. It is up to you to go back, by whatever means you can, over the ground you covered in that time. No, don't interrupt. I can give you no advice further than to say: *Think where you have been.* You have some sharpness, Jessica; use it now."

"I don't know what it looks like."

"Probably not as it should. Otherwise it would have been discovered long ago. Had such a precious object as the Plate of Alquar shone in its true colours it would have been treasured in your world as much as in ours. Even if none of your people could guess its power, they would have valued it instinctively. If you have the privilege of touching it you will soon know it for what it is."

"What should I do?"

"Bring it to us here."

"Yes, but — "

"Oh you mean how do you get there and back? I will show you when we go outside. You can only leave and enter through one of Magob's gates so remember well when I tell you where these are placed. When they close, as they are beginning to do now, we shall be separated from you forever."

"But Ann. . .Peter. . ."

Duguth shook his head and replied: "Eat Jessica, for you have the busiest day of your life ahead of you."

"I can't," said Jessica again. "Not leave Ann and Peter. Not go alone."

"Listen," said Duguth. "They have faced their challenge. What has happened may be no one's fault. The Plate of Alquar bears four figures, and though we have planned one way, if it must be another then it is provided for. I as a Glyph may not make this journey, for the search belongs in your world. You are the only one left who can do it."

"But — I ran away — "

"I know," said Duguth rising to brush this last plea aside. "You would have had some protection if you had faced the Shadow. We can do nothing about that now. You must go even without."

Duguth's tone forbade further argument. In surly temper Jessica followed instructions from moment to moment. The older woman furrowed her brow as she watched Annis fasten her son's cloak once more about the girl's neck. Then Jessica stepped outside into the freshness of dawn, glad more than anything to escape this grim house.

"Nephew," said Duguth's aunt, retaining him, "you made a great fuss about this Shadow as you call it. The girl has not gone through with the test. What will happen to her?"

"Should she ever lay hands on the Plate there will be great danger. We must let things take their course."

He turned and followed Jessica into the air. They went past yards where cocks crowed and pigs snorted up from sleep. Then out into a countryside where the remainder of last season's harvest still strewed the fields.

There were questions Jessica wanted to ask but couldn't frame. So many of them, and time was running out.

Duguth addressed her very quietly and patiently.

"Jessica," he said, "should you — I say rather, *when* you

have the Plate of Alquar in your grasp, take great care. It will link you with Gwynod and with the other half. You have not yet come to terms with your Shadow and will have no protection when Magob stretches out to you. Just for now, though, forget these things. It is better to go without fear. Set your mind on what you have to do and shut out all else. Are you ready?"

"Yes," said Jessica tight-lipped and surprised at herself. There were hundreds of things not said — not asked.

"Then we are coming to the gate where you entered Gwynod. Give me your cloak. You will have no need of it where you are going and I will keep it for when you return."

Jessica slipped the cloak reluctantly from her shoulders and shivered. They were close to a barbarous-looking hedge.

"There is a path through there," said Duguth.

Jessica walked on but, suddenly aware that Duguth's steps were not following, she turned. Duguth stood watching but everything about him was growing faint.

"Duguth," called Jessica, and she knew he answered her for she could see his lips move. Only there was no voice but her own in the summer air.

As Duguth watched Jessica's startled face fade from sight he spoke to give her courage, but he knew she could no longer hear. Very soon there was only the rough hedgerow in front of him. The early cawing of field birds arose. He wondered whether their special awareness could bridge the two worlds that were so close at this moment of time. Did they fly with two bodies — one here and one in that other place?

His mind filled with conflict as he strode back to Pengaron. He had established himself as a leader among the Glyphs. He had planned and worked for this moment. Even the Venerable Ones had been brought to listen to him. Yet it was a mere chit of a girl who must perform the most dangerous part of the exploit, something she neither understood nor wanted.

Brooding sombrely on these things he reached Pengaron as Peter came stumbling towards him up the road from the coast.

"Peter," exclaimed Duguth aghast. Had he really sent Jessica out on a mission which in another half-hour she need not have undertaken?

Once again, but in different tones, Duguth said: "Peter." He walked quickly towards the boy and grasped hold of him. Peter swayed, and Duguth with an arm round his shoulder drew him straight into the village. The place had the stirring of a new day about it. Keith and Marran met them with pails, staring curiously from raw, scrubbed faces as Duguth led his companion indoors.

Peter collapsed into a chair and whispered: "I made it."

He waited for Duguth to say: "As I expected", but the acknowledgement did not come. Only Annis and her mother fussed over him.

"I'm all right," he said stoutly. "And the cloak."

He touched it to draw Annis's attention to the care he had taken. She smiled in return.

"Where's Ann and Jess?" he asked looking round.

Duguth came and sat next to him. Then while Peter swallowed soup he explained the position affairs had come to in his absence.

Ann in Caer Owen? Peter clutched involuntarily at his arm. And Jessica performing his mission? What a fool he'd been. They'd gone in search of him. That was like Ann — she'd never let you down.

"If you had come half an hour sooner — " said Duguth.

An ember of resentment glowed in Peter. He had thought himself into the job of Plate-finder. Yet the quest had gone after all to a girl. He swallowed very hard and said with a new strength and a new understanding in him: "Who knows, she might do better."

"She has not come through the ordeal with the Shadow,"

129

said Duguth. "Quickness will not be enough. I am afraid she will flow like water whichever way Magob puffs upon her."

"But *Ann*," said Peter.

Ann in Caer Owen. Ann locked in with the Boujacks. Pain wrenched at his shoulder.

"There is something wrong with your arm," said Duguth who had been watching him closely.

"My arm's all right," said Peter brusquely.

"Your shoulder it must be then."

"Not — exactly — "

Peter's face burned when he thought of the tell-tale mark. To be labelled in such a way! He did not wish either Duguth or Annis to know about it.

"You have been hurt," said Duguth. "I *must* look."

Peter's lips locked mulishly.

"Come outside," said the man, "and we will walk."

The morning was calm after the high wind of the previous night, and there was crisp frost in the air. They walked peacefully down the path leading in the direction of the sea. Duguth made no attempt to speed their journey or to draw on the power of the road to carry them to any destination. When they had gone a distance from the village, he said:

"You have some wound, Peter. That is evident. I don't ask you to tell me everything that has happened in Caer Owen if you prefer not to but I must know why your left arm is a subject of torment to you. That is my responsibility."

Reluctantly Peter told Duguth about events after his encounter with the Shadow: his imprisonment by the Boujacks throughout the night; and the things he had seen in the castle. Then with bitter loathing he allowed Duguth to uncover his inflamed shoulder. To his astonishment the man solemnly said:

"In one respect we have made no mistake. Jessica was the only choice for the quest."

130

Peter stared at him.

"You see," said Duguth, "the Boujacks punctured your skin so that Magob might have a tag on you. It is a pity it had to happen but you feel worse about it than you need. It would have put you and us in great danger had you gone with that mark on you after the Plate of Alquar. I understand why Magob allowed you to leave Caer Owen. He knew that the quest had been assigned to you. He was curious, but he could not get all the information he needed. Which must mean that Ann has revealed nothing about the object we seek. Through that imprint on your arm he can track you whenever it pleases him. He would know before you touched the Plate that that was your goal."

"The flowers — and the plants — " exclaimed Peter.

"Oh yes, we know about them. The Glyphs buy from the Boujacks only to put in their stew pots. Magob is always seeking to enter our homes, but we remain a practical people."

"Can he hear us now?" asked Peter.

"No, you will know when he seeks to contact you. The mark on your shoulder will burn very bright; it will cause you discomfort perhaps, but only so as to irritate. You may find yourself forgetting why your arm itches at times. But look well and you will see I am right. Then be very careful what you say and what you think."

Peter was silent for some time, glancing every now and then at his shoulder. He could feel nothing except an ache, and certainly the mark was less noticeable than it had been. He wondered if he could disguise it when he went swimming.

At last he said: "It's a clever kind of thing, isn't it? Sort of inventive you know. I wouldn't have thought it would be possible in your time. Now, I mean."

"When do you think *now* is?" asked Duguth.

Peter was perplexed. Like Ann he supposed, from the way people dressed and lived, that they had slipped back in time to — somewhere round the Dark Ages.

"Why should you imagine," Duguth asked, "that we have anything to do with the *past*?"

They came out in view of the bay, the dark weight of Caer Owen brooding distantly to the north. Peter wondered how many times he had tramped that road between Pengaron and the sea. Yet walking it with Duguth in the morning light was different from his limping fear-ridden trek of last night.

The tide was advancing once more, the coastal rocks waiting peacefully dry as yet.

"I have time," said Duguth, "to cross to Caer Owen and open the tunnel. It may be that Ann has returned and is waiting just within for us to move. You must rest here while I am gone. You are missing your sleep."

"I'd rather come along," said Peter.

"I know, but it will be better if I go alone. If Ann is not there I can remain until the very last moment the sea allows. Look, there is dry grass that will be comfortable. Lie down on your cloak and doze if you can. We neither of us know what we may have to face before the day is over."

Peter knew that if it weren't for the freshness of the air he would drop with exhaustion. As he looked round he thought he caught a glimpse of the Venerable Ones already in position on Gullzin.

"Why do they watch there?" he asked.

"They watch Caer Owen always," said Duguth. "Not as the Boujacks watch us, in a spying manner. But rather as part of an old tradition. While the watchers remain on Gullzin we may still link with the Cenarti and at the same time assert the strength of our will against Magob."

"But when the tide comes in," said Peter, "they don't stay on Gullzin then?"

"No, they retire to Pengaron. As they do also when dusk falls. But we are glad for what effort they are able to make."

Duguth stalked ahead and Peter turned to where the yellow bank of grass tempted him to stretch out. He slept peacefully until the tide had crept well into the bay and Duguth was back at his side.

Peter started up, wondering at the brightness of light around him. The day was further advanced but there was no sign of Ann.

"What d'you *think* has happened?" he asked, sitting up cross-legged.

"I don't know," said Duguth morosely. "We must wait again for the tide to turn."

The size of all rocks was shrinking as the water submerged their lower parts. Only Gullzin still rose impressively to face the massive fort at the other side of the bay. The Venerables had waded ashore but whether they had gone home or were squatting further along the cliff Peter couldn't make out.

"Our hopes depend on Jessica," said Duguth.

"You know," said Peter, "she'll be lost when it comes to looking for the Plate. I'd have been too. It's a rotten task you've set her."

Duguth made no answer.

The waves were licking the cliff quite leisurely today. The man and boy sat watching them as if they had all the time in the world. Peter yielded to the mesmeric calm, thinking idly how like a crab's pincers the two headlands looked at either end of the bay. Or bandy legs, he thought — for the curve was really quite distinct. A giant's bandy legs, he decided, the curve was so extensive.

Then Duguth was on his feet, gazing fixedly out to sea.

Peter looked up at him, wanting to ask: "What is it?" but the man's appearance alarmed him. He scrambled up and peered too. Both of them stood rooted to the spot while what they were watching happened very slowly.

"They're closing," said Duguth in the phantom of a whisper. "The gates are closing."

The two stretches of land had come round in a huge arc.

Their stature seemed to diminish as the tide poured through, but it was distance only that made them look slight. Peter knew that close-to they would be powerful, barren, solid rock, nested in by gulls.

And they were moving. They were coming together as once before they had appeared capable of doing. This time, however, Peter could see that they were going to complete the circle. The watery bay would be cut off from the ocean without.

"What does it mean?" cried Peter.

"If they shut tight," said Duguth, "the other gates will be doing the same and Jessica will have no way back to us. I should not have let you leave the village. Magob knows now from his spies that you are not the one who has been sent; that he has been cheated of the first advantage if not of the last. So he is making certain before anything threatens that no one can enter Gwynod."

"It can't happen," cried Peter, almost shaking his fists at the water. Within the bay there was less of a tide than before. Only in the centre, as the sea spurted through the remaining gap, was the moon still pulling against Magob's increasing advantage.

Then as they watched, a great surge sounded.

Ann had listened very carefully to Duguth when he told the story of his father's intrusion into Caer Owen. So she was prepared for all the difficulties and discouragements that the wall-set spiral brought. It was dark for long intervals. It was airless in those intervals to the point of suffocation. The chalky odour clawed at her throat.

Every now and then came the relief of a window slit with its breath of sea-freshness and its dart of light. Opposite each slit Ann could make out a squat door etched spidery on the wall. She touched none of them, but continued to ascend.

When she reached the topmost bend she was crawling like Duguth's father with exhaustion and dizziness, but she found less difficulty in squeezing her slight frame right up until she could strike at the roof above. She remembered, too late, that the door would open onto a hearth and there was every likelihood at this time of year that a fire would be burning.

The roof creaked as her fist hit on the spring. It swung back with neither flame nor logs in sight, and Ann heaved herself up into chill spaciousness.

She blinked through smirched glasses at a room whose light was shaded, though it seemed glaring enough to her after the darkness she had emerged from. It was so quiet that the place must be deserted.

In the centre of the room, however, was a tall, carved chair, facing downwards towards the window. As Ann approached it slowly from behind she could see that a very old man sat there. She stopped, terrified partly for his sake, in case he experienced some terrible shock if she spoke to him or made herself known as a stranger. Perhaps he was asleep — she couldn't tell — though his head was quite erect.

What shall I do? wondered Ann, standing absolutely still. Then a voice came from the chair — a thin, silvery sound.

"Who are you that have come within the sphere of my thinking? There is a place for the young as there is for the old. You were instructed to stay there."

"I — I — I would like to talk to you," said Ann, trying to give the same dignity to her tone as that which came through the old man's.

"Talk — do we talk any longer?"

They were strange words and Ann did not understand them. But she was intent on finding a way to introduce herself.

"I am not Cenarti," she said outright, feeling it better to confess early rather than late.

Silence followed. Ann wondered if she had frightened the old one, but his head had not dropped in any way.

She stepped quietly round the chair. The old man had seemed bald from the back but she could see now that his high-domed forehead was haloed with sparse white hair that came down the side of his cheeks to flow more fully at the chin. As soon as she entered his vision his eyes followed her round. He had the boniness of age about him, even though a long robe hooded most of his body. Ann's attention was drawn to the strange shapes that were deeply patterned round the hem and on the sleeves.

"I am not Cenarti," she said again timidly, hoping that the full sight of her would remedy any shock he might have felt.

There was something about him that was both pathetic and haughty. Ann trembled a little as she came under the power of his scrutiny.

"You are not a Boujack," he said at length. "They would not dare in any case — " He paused to take a breath. "It happened, once, a long time ago, that a non-Cenarti came to steal from us."

"Steal!" exclaimed Ann, who immediately connected the non-Cenarti with Duguth's father.

"He stole from our ancient stock. He carried my sister from us."

Had he said "daughter" Ann would have thought it equally possible, for the man seemed ancient indeed. Only his eyes had a peculiar brilliance and the dome of his head was unwrinkled.

"What does a stranger want with us?"

"To remind you," said Ann, groping to understand her purpose in coming here.

"Of the man who stole from us?" asked the elder.

"Of the Glyphs."

"Such a word is not familiar in these halls. I recall that the other stranger used it; but it is not welcome here."

"I am not a Glyph," cried Ann. "But still I want you to remember."

"We are too tired to remember," said the Ancient One petulantly. "What shall we remember, we who have had so much to fill our thoughts? If one small thing is forgotten in the midst of all knowledge what does it signify?"

Ideas were coming fast into Ann's head.

"Well," she said, "if you lost one small key you might not get into lots of big rooms. It depends *what* you forget."

"An Ancient One does not need teaching," said the man authoritatively. "Look around you, stranger. Feast your senses on our genius, see what we have aspired to, and tell me was it not worth losing the world for such a dream?"

He dropped back exhausted into his chair while Ann turned automatically to do as he had bidden. She could almost recognise the long tapestries. Like Duguth's father she saw the great forests that lined the walls, the deer and the sunlight and the sweeping foliage. But the gold threads did not shine, and the colours had faded.

She wandered back to the old man and saw that his eyes were glinting more sharply than any gold in the artefacts around. He had been watching her closely as she moved about the room.

"I will call my people," he said, "and you will see still more."

There was a greedy jealousy in his voice as if he craved admiration for the Cenarti's achievement. Ann watched him place long gnarled hands on each of the lion heads at the corners of his chair and close his eyes. Intensity gripped all his features as he drew others to the great page doors at the end of the hall. Three people entered softly, a man and two young women.

"Take her round," ordered the Ancient One, "and

round, and round — until she understands her own insignificance."

So Ann went among the Cenarti as Peter had gone among the Boujacks.

The young women, Ann noticed, had more an air about them to suggest oldness than youth. All the Cenarti wore long white robes and Ann asked about the strange signs that ran along the edge of these.

"On mine," said one, "are symbols for each of the metallic elements."

"On mine," said the other, "are the shapes of orbits of planets in our solar system."

"On both there are signs that stand for inner mysteries, secrets of beauty and order in the universe."

They returned their explanation pit-a-pat, a trifle weary of the trouble it cost them. Ann understood nothing except that it was very learned and even if they had explained it to her she would never be able to follow. The phrase "inner mysteries", however, she liked.

They passed other Cenarti, all of them tall, stately, and hardly impressed by Ann's presence. Everybody, she noticed, had a certain weariness, as if their minds were long since surfeited with the things they knew.

The halls were all draped to keep out too much light. Ann compared the people with flowers that grew tall and spindly in the shade. Many of them had dome-shaped heads, the men shaving their fine hair at the back to follow the style of the Ancient One. Their whiskers made them look older than they were and tended to run to silver early. Ann thought of the Glyphs by contrast: their clean-shaven faces, their stockiness from the hips down, their stamping eager communication with the earth under their feet.

That the Cenarti had surrounded themselves with everything their creative ingenious minds could invent was clear. All was of the finest: leather, silver, gold. But there was a

138

tremendous strangeness worked into each object that was above ordinary craftsmanship.

They entered a room where the most ancient of their treasures were kept. These belonged to the days when the Cenarti had been warriors. Ann saw breast plates with etched symbols, pattern-welded swords and daggers, helmets linked to natural magic with animal figures. There was power coursing through them all. She could feel it.

The Cenarti themselves, Ann noticed, observed all things in a bored, leisurely way. Earlier artists had depicted animals, birds, fish and forests. Later ones played with shapes and mathematical designs that meant little to her.

"I like the oldest things best," she said.

"We are an ancient people," came the polite answer.

"What is happening *now*?" asked Ann.

They shook their heads with casual grace and said: "Have we not shown you enough?"

They returned to where the Ancient One still clutched at the heads of old lions.

"Well," he demanded, "did you see how our men of science plot the movement of the heavens?"

"I didn't understand it," admitted Ann.

"And the books our learned men have compiled? Did you go to our room of music?"

"It was very weird."

"The secrets of the universe that we have learned and studied would mean nothing to you," said the old man striking one of the carved heads.

"I think all the best things were done years ago," said Ann.

The old man leaned back in his chair. She could see his throat move convulsively as he tried to answer her.

"We have work to do for our Taskmaster," he said grievingly. "He has commanded too much of recent years. So much we have given already. Yet he accuses us of holding back our discoveries. He wearies me with the pull he exerts. I feel it fastening on me here."

139

The man raised his hands and clutched, wide-fingered, at his head.

"You mean Magob?" said Ann.

"It is an old word, that we do not use these days," said the Ancient One, "but I remember that it had some meaning. The Boujacks are his people. We despised them for a long time and thought that he was no more than they are. But we were wrong."

The man sank into lethargy and Ann felt as if she had come to the end of what she could do. What was the point of Peter searching for the Plate of Alquar, what was the use of Duguth's planning, and the Venerables watching from Gullzin, if such were the Cenarti?

She wandered back down the room to where a thin brightness filtered through curtains. Ann remembered that all the Cenarti side of Caer Owen was towards the sea. Before she could look, however, her attention was caught by another brightness, an object tucked away in a corner, between window and tapestry where no light could fall. Yet it seemed to have a peculiar radiance of its own. She went closer, blinking as was her custom. Somehow it had the oddest of shapes. . .

"So you have come here to steal too," spat a voice so close to Ann's ear and so full of viperish wrath that her heart jumped as she turned to face the speaker. The old man she had left sunk in his chair was a towering, terrible figure of judgement.

What had excited him? She dragged away from those mesmeric, furious eyes and turned again to the wall. She knew, she knew, she knew. Hadn't she seen it months ago in the gypsy's tent?

"It's — "

She gasped as she looked full at the object. It was minutes before she could speak but when she did she said:

"Not to steal, but to tell you about the other half."

Ann thought that if she stayed a century with the Cenarti

she could not feel sadder than she did at this moment. Not the ancient ones, not the young Cenarti, not a man or woman had enough in them to answer the challenge.

"The Glyphs are seeking the other half of the Plate," she had told them. "They have pledged to restore it to you. The old wounds can be healed and they will unite with you once again."

Why shouldn't they throw off the bondage of Magob? If she had been able to climb to them by the secret spiral they could go out the same way.

"We are Cenarti," said the Ancient One proudly, "and we entered by the grand stairway. Our Taskmaster knew what befitted us. Shall we creep forth like dogs?"

Ann began to understand how Magob had gained a hold over these people. She got up again from beside the old man's chair and walked to the window, determined this time to reach the air. She slipped out onto a narrow parapet. As far as the eye could see was an expanse of slate-grey water with no longer any beach in sight. Only the far prongs of the bay were dark shapes on the horizon.

She wasn't sure how long she stood examining the world's width before she became aware of what was happening. As the rocky headlands drew together the sea rushed frantically through the enclosing pincers. Magob was shutting out the sea. He had power to do so. . . .power over water.

What was it Duguth had said about gates closing? They had to get hold of the Plate before that happened or it would be too late.

Words echoed in Ann's head. Power over water. Power over water. The Power of Water, Duguth had said in reference to herself.

She concentrated on that inpouring tide, feeling its drench and turmoil as it became blocked in its customary course. It was fighting hard now, shock-beating at all obstacles as Ann called upon it to win, to win. Not to let Magob get away with what he was doing. Not to make it too late. Whoever had gone in search of the Plate of Alquar must have the chance to return.

The vision of Magob's fortress that Ann had seen in the stream came forcibly to her mind. There were tides rising inside her as she called on the water to prevail.

The sea came with a great surge, rising from its bed higher than the land mass, sweeping across encroaching rock with a hideous snarl. Then as it crashed toward the fort the spray rose and Ann saw the great eagle-flighted sea like a curtain above her, enclosing the Cenarti and Magob and all Magob's men, swallowing the whole of Caer Owen.

"It's Ann's doing," called Duguth, as he and Peter watched the billowing wave make straight for the fortress.

He dragged Peter to the nearest clump of trees for support, spray-drenched and blinded.

"Ann," cried Peter. "Ann."

As the mist cleared he ran forward to the cliff edge.

"Come back," called Duguth. "There's nothing you can do."

The water had subsided and only a quicker swirling told of disturbance. Peter gazed horror-struck along the bay towards the rock from which the fort should rise. It was as empty as if Magob had never been.

"Ann," whispered Peter.

"Don't you understand?" said Duguth coming up behind and putting his hand on the boy's shoulder. "She has used the Power of Water to do this. She has stopped Magob from closing his gates — for a while at least. Look."

He directed Peter to see how the headland points had returned to their normal position. The bay lay open to the incoming tide.

"But Caer Owen," said Peter in bewilderment. "Where's it gone?"

"She has taken the fort beneath the waves," said Duguth. "The power is against Magob until the sea in the

142

bay retreats. I fear it will hold no longer than that, but it may give Jessica time."

"Will Ann be all right?"

Duguth made no answer.

"Tell me."

"I don't know," he admitted. "She is human and the force is great and elemental. The water will give us answers in its own time."

"You mean," said Peter, "she could be drowned."

"She has decided the matter for herself and we must wait."

A thought crossed Peter's mind.

"Where are the Watchers who should be on Gullzin?" he demanded.

Duguth stared.

"You know they went long since."

Peter turned, muttering between clenched teeth: "Then I will watch."

He ran south round the cliff edge in the direction of Gullzin. After an impulse to follow, Duguth let him go. He understood the boy's feeling, and it could be that each of them was now finding his true part in this pattern of Alquar.

Peter knew he would have to wade out to Gullzin. He scrambled down the path, lichen-edged, that the Venerable Ones used in their descent to the beach. He measured the distance Gullzin lay ahead before he entered the water. It looked, from sea level, much further off than it did from the cliff top. He pushed hard against the flurrying tide.

The water was round his waist as he reached the rock. A passing thought for Annis's cloak made him wind it high on his shoulders; he would not abandon it, cumbersome though it was. It would hardly spoil with wetting. He found footholds on the sharp-sided rock and crawled clammily up.

There was more sea to come, and at very high tide he knew the rock would be virtually covered. But the Captain's words came back to him, heard at a time when he was green in stomach, about the tip of the rock always protruding in the very deepest water.

He must trust to that. Finding a niche near the rock summit he lodged himself tight against the wind. Then he began squeezing out the cloak.

Peter knew he would have a lengthy wait, and that it could become painful. He gazed steadily across the bay at where the fort was no longer to be seen. He would maintain the link which the Watchers kept with the Cenarti; and he wouldn't let Ann go through this on her own.

Duguth waited a long time on the cliff side. He watched Peter's journey and arrival; he imagined a little what it must be like clinging wet to the rough perch while the tide swelled.

The Glyphs had no liking for the sea, Duguth had once said. He had little taste for it himself. The Cenarti on the other hand were drawn to the ways of water far more than to the tending of the soil. When they broke with the Glyphs they went shorewards to reach Caer Owen. What could have seemed a more fitting refuge than that which pinioned them on the brink of the ocean?

Duguth concentrated hard on Peter, trying to watch with him, but not entirely sure what he hoped to accomplish. The boy had presumably learnt something from his experience in Caer Owen. What Duguth did know was that the tide was rising. Every minute the flow strengthened.

He wondered what Peter's chances were of swimming ashore. The water would carry him but there were rocks. . .

Peter however did not stir from Gullzin. Duguth could just make out his head. The boy must be covered up to the shoulders and the water would be slapping its way across his face.

Suddenly he saw movement. Peter's head was trying to come up further. But it was a useless attempt. He couldn't climb on top of the jagged points. Nor, Duguth believed, could he cling there for long if he left the shelter of his cranny. Duguth held his breath. What was the boy planning to do?

Peter knew he mustn't see or think of anything except Caer Owen and Ann-within-the-fortress. The water around held Ann, and he was in it with her. He had long forgotten the feel of his limbs, but they didn't matter anyway, for his job was to watch. His watery world was a capricious place, sometimes heaving high above him, sometimes sucking right down. But this time he wouldn't go ill or green. When the Captain called he would reel the line and take the tiller as bidden, and lanky Glyn Evans would be stretched out in the bottom of the boat, and together they'd reel in Ann and all her castles.

Peter wondered if he did feel sick, but dismissed the notion. His mind must be wandering to imagine a thing like that.

He discovered that it would be no good releasing himself from his niche. The odds against his holding on were too great. If he should be flooded out he would have to swim for the shore and that would be dangerous even with the present soft tide. Besides, he doubted now if he had the use of his limbs.

He was practising holding his breath at intervals as the water splashed over his face. The raining spray gave almost no breathing space between. Peter thought of Ann and how the sea had washed right over Caer Owen. He had to concentrate. He had to breathe for her. He had to *see* the fort still standing on its rock.

Peter knew that the moment was close when the water would swirl right over his frozen body and not retreat. He had raised his head as far as he could from his wedged-in position.

He gasped as the memories came and went. Duguth had said they could each of them use an elemental Power. Ann

145

had called on the Power of Water, he said, and the water had come. Now at this moment Peter chose Air.

It was air he needed, both for himself and for Ann. Hadn't he taken up his position on Gullzin in order to be a lifeline?

As the last wave burst over him Peter called, soundlessly, on the Power of Air. The water arched and dropped, rising still on either side but leaving him a clear channel through which to blink and draw breath. Pain dispersed slowly from his nostrils and lungs. Peter found that no more waves came near his face. The rest of him was still trapped, but he could breathe easily, sweetly, and he could see ahead all the way to the rock of Caer Owen.

To her astonishment Jessica felt incredibly hot. She un-peeled her cardigan and blinked at the hedge which was thick and brambly. Over to the right ran the road, its haze almost too bright to look at.

It was summer, and she had come through the hedge and out onto the road. Further up she could see the end of the station wall. Jessica gasped, partly with the relief familiar things always brought, partly with the shock of knowing two different existences in the same moment.

A boy passing on a bicycle glanced back at her standing alone by the hedge. Jessica bent and pulled at her socks. Then she marched resolutely forward as if the station were her goal.

People were crossing into it by the wicket gate, which

meant there must be a train due. The women were in flowery, home-cut dresses, and they were accompanied by children neatly arrayed for a day's visit to town. It can't still be Saturday, thought Jessica incredulously. Then she recognised some of the crowd on the platform and gasped again. Everything was just as she and Peter and Ann had left it when they strolled down the road. It *must* be Saturday. There was a train due for Abertowyn, and this was a last-shopping, last-spree occasion before school started.

Jessica thought quickly what it meant. The Pinchers would not be searching for them. Nothing in fact had happened between setting out that morning for a picnic and standing here on Duffryn platform. Nothing, that was, except that she was alone.

Her mind hovered, half in this summer's day in Duffryn, and half in the autumn of Gwynod. The crowd around was chattering mainly in Welsh, which made her feel more of a stranger now than she had done in the other place. Here she was, warm in the sun, while Keith and Marran had the lengthening nights of winter to look forward to.

She tried hard to draw back into the present, to concentrate on what lay around. But the present was a blank without Ann and Peter. A train came and Jessica boarded it automatically along with the others.

"What am I doing?" she asked herself. The answer was ridiculous — searching for the Plate of Alquar. "It's nonsense really," she tried to make herself think, but only ten minutes ago she had been with Duguth. He had said that she (or the others) had been near the Plate some time during the previous week.

Jessica knew that their visit to Abertowyn was the only occasion when they had been together outside the area she thought of now as "Magob's territory".

She settled back into her seat and watched fields and hills trickle by. At one point everybody craned forward to look at where the goods train had been derailed the previous day.

"There was no need for it, man," said one.

A woman with a little boy in the compartment spoke Welsh to her as if trying to make up for the fact that the girl was on her own.

When the inspector came down the train Jessica remembered she didn't have a ticket. She dug into her skirt pocket and snatched at its contents. The crisp one-pound note that was her father's last indulgence was still secure in its tiny purse. She stared at it. Had it really lain there all the time she'd been with Annis and Duguth and in the tunnel at Caer Owen?

The man beamed as she handed him her fare.

"Sent you out for the day, girl?" he asked. "Got a bit of work to do in town?"

Jessica smiled but she didn't answer, though he addressed her in English. These people were wanting to know about her, she reckoned, but she wasn't going to tell them. *Careless talk costs lives.* She took her change and counted it back into its holder. It looked much more this way. She wished the threepenny bit had been a silver one. Then she remembered Ann's, lying where she'd pushed it in her hanky. Special, Ann had called it.

The time passed. They drew into Abertowyn while she was still debating with herself: What am I going to do? Where do I go first?

The woman said something again, friendly-like, and Jessica nodded, hoping that the Welsh didn't require an answer. Then she walked straight towards the ticket barrier as if she was quite sure where she was going, out of the station and up the road they had all gone with Miss Jones on the day Peter visited his new school.

"It's ridiculous," she thought. "I'm being rushed all the time. I've got to slow down and think."

Could visit Peter's school. Could visit Woolworth's. Could visit the museum. Could look in the tea shop they'd stopped at before catching the train home. Could look at several other shops on the way. Jessica eliminated the

148

lavatories, and the bench where she and Ann had stopped to eat their sandwiches outside the museum.

The trouble was that she wasn't sure that any of these places was right. It must be inside somewhere, she thought, then asked herself why. Since it had been flung out of Gwynod it could be lying around on any old dust heap or under some hedge. But Duguth had said that it must have been picked up and carried off because it lay well outside the circle.

Jessica thought hard. She was quick at noticing things, though what they meant didn't always register with her. Ann was better at perceiving connections.

She decided to follow the same route as last time. She reached the top of the slope, was signalled across two main roads by white-armed policemen, and glanced at some of the shops on the way. To Jessica they were mainly dull places, like bicycle stores. The Plate, she was sure, wouldn't be there. Perhaps a china shop now. . .

Jessica wished, not for the first time, that she knew what it looked like. Vaguely she understood what pattern to expect. It would be part of a broken circle that had four figures, representing the corners of a square. A circle and a square. *Mandala* was what Duguth called it. Well, two figures at least should be clear on it.

Suppose someone had tried restoring it? It might not even be the shape she was looking for. Jessica had seen old plates — a great-aunt of hers had several — where the china was riveted at the back by a metal pin. It didn't seem to matter that all kinds of cracks were present. Great Aunt Maria had two on the wall of her passage, and very proud she was of them. In the same way Mrs. Pincher took loving care of her willow-pattern china. Jessica couldn't recall noticing if any of it had been broken, but she was sure Mrs. Pincher was just the person to find a way of repairing it. Perhaps someone like her had found the Plate of Alquar and "restored" it by anchoring another bit to it. They'd have to do a good job if it was to appear a whole plate.

With ideas like these Jessica teased herself until she came to the point where she thought they had turned off the main thoroughfare. She was now in a street of small grocers, a fishmonger, and other shops.

A tiny woman with very noticeable bow legs called out as she passed: "A bit of the old-fashioned this," glancing up at the sky.

Jessica said pleasantly: "Isn't it!" and walked on.

They always said that you could get lost in a crowd, but she was finding it singularly difficult. On any other occasion Jessica would have responded to friendliness, but just today, when she didn't want to be noticed. . . .

She turned into a road that was mainly offices, and hesitated. Somewhere in this direction was the square with the museum and library. That was where Miss Jones had taken them as being a safe and interesting place, and from where they had wandered back among the traffic and found Woolworths.

By dint of persistent meandering Jessica came into Tudor Square and saw the dignified features of public buildings with their regulated flower beds. She wondered if she should go straight back to the shops.

The museum itself presented a problem. It was unknown territory since she hadn't gone into it on the first occasion. On the other hand, Ann had. Besides, it was the most obvious place to look for an old broken bit of plate. Jessica wondered what she would do if she sighted the Plate of Alquar sealed under glass.

Wouldn't it be better to go first to the places she had actually been herself? There was the cinema and the shops and — Patsy Doyle of course. Ann had behaved badly there, Jessica decided, going off like that and leaving her to find her own way to the square. She had clung on to Patsy as long as she could, saying: "Just go to the *next* corner with me." Until Patsy had revolted and pushed off home for dinner.

Ann had also complicated things by adding the museum

150

to the list of places to be searched. Jessica stood undecided. It frightened her more now, and she would have to go past the uniformed attendants all on her own.

Yet somehow her feet wouldn't let her escape the way she wanted. She was crossing beside the library with the Saturday stack of bikes outside, to its sister building, with benches, garden, and that absurd statue. She walked slowly along to the place she and Ann had sat, and plumped down. She was tired with walking — it had been quite a pull up from the station — and Jessica had no refreshment with her this time. She wondered idly what to do about food.

A chap further along was sitting with his back half to her, legs crossed slouchingly in the other direction. Jessica felt the sun draw her into laziness. It was from here that she and Ann had gazed at the statue with the fauns dancing, cloven-footed at its corners, and giggled at the nudity of the Discus Thrower.

Four fauns, said Jessica to herself. Like the Plate with its four figures. She wondered if one of the figures on the Plate actually looked like her. She got up to examine the fauns.

They were sculpted into perpetual laughter, some secret rocking their bodies with grotesque merriment. By contrast the Discus Thrower was intense and serious, his mind removed from all distraction.

He's in another world, thought Jessica. They don't belong to it.

Then she sighed and turned to face the museum. Up the wide low steps. Four, she counted. Then into the dusky entrance where an elderly man in custodian's outfit sat quietly watching people enter and leave. Jessica tried, as she had done since the station at Duffryn, to look as if she knew where she wanted to go. She walked straight forward into the room of Roman remains.

There seemed an awful lot of them, especially when you had to glance at each item in turn; so many dishes that time and use and burial had distorted. Fortunately she felt no temptation to read the information attached to the glass cases. It was a shape she was after.

Another thing she didn't know was the size of the Plate. Jessica felt cross that she hadn't asked Duguth about that, it was such an obviously necessary bit of information. Was it dinner-plate size, or tea-plate size?

She imagined that it was some kind of china or pottery substance she was after, but she remembered Duguth saying that no one believed it could ever be broken. Why shouldn't it be gold or silver then? You couldn't break that by dropping it. Yet the fact remained that it *had* split.

The thoughts flew like birds through her head. She had to concentrate, like the Discus Thrower, in the face of distraction.

She came to a whole section of faience pottery, its glaze like a hard stare from the walls around. As she moved down the room she felt it bearing in on her as a focal point. It came into her mind that she knew about the corners of the Plate, *but not the centre*.

What was at the heart of a ring of four?

Jessica halted. Something was nagging in her head like a pin being driven through. She *had* to find out.

She turned and would have raced out of the museum had she not been restrained by the watchful calm of its guardians. Once she reached the steps, however, she flew.

The man was still sitting on his bench further up, looking in another direction. Jessica went back to the little statuary group that was set into one corner of the lawn. She stepped onto the grass to walk round.

In a way the artist had mocked public taste by putting together such different things. The Discus Thrower didn't belong to the world of the fauns. They were mythical, fantastic beings, behaving with the licence of their creator. Whereas the man himself was a true-to-life, well-proportioned athlete, projecting his superb human skill into the throw of the disc.

There *is* something wrong about it, thought Jessica, puzzling hard to understand.

She let her feet rest on the grass and bent her body into the same position as the athlete. The great weighty disc was held underarm, the strong fingers steadying and poising it along the rim. He had raised it so high behind that the front part of his torso was in line with the sides of his legs. Everything was geared to the final roll.

Jessica felt it was now she needed to know. The earth came to life like a power dynamo beneath her feet. She crouched, knees angled, body twisted, as she balanced the disc in the straight of her right forearm.

The Power of Earth flowed through Jessica and she grew tall as the man and saw around her the imp-faces that held her in their ring. The disc was firm in her hand, its great central weight upheld by the energy surging through the girl.

It was then that Jessica knew what it was she held. The riveting bond ran through her arm.

As the earth's power sank away she felt her slight body released from its tension. She was her own size and she held nothing. But she understood what she had to do.

She chose the shady side of the statue. With a vault through the ring of fauns, she was up to the man and steadying herself with one hand on his back-stretched arm. Then she took hold of the lower half of the disc. Her senses told her it was stone. Heavy, immoveable, smooth grey stone. Very firmly she pulled. Releasing her grip on the statue's arm she caught in both hands the piece that came away.

It was no longer stone as she held it now, but something heavier and finer at the same time, and *affecting*. A tremendous poignancy stole through Jessica as if she stood on the threshold of great sorrow, a visitor at a house of mourning.

She stepped swiftly out from the circle of gaping fauns. With the Plate of Alquar clutched to her middle

153

she looked guiltily round to see if anyone was watching.

The man on his bench had turned towards her. How long had she been within his scrutiny? She moved away from the stone figures, pretending to be at ease. Someone must notice soon that the athlete balanced impossibly in the hollow of his arm only one half of a disc.

Jessica glanced towards the library. For a brief moment it had been quiet. Now there seemed to be people swarming all over. A crowd of boys appeared but they were concentrating on unstacking their bikes.

She glanced up at windows. A hundred spies that she knew nothing of. Would they bother about a girl clambering up a statue? Jessica decided it was time to make off.

She tried as she walked to conceal her new treasure but its size defeated her. It must be nearly a foot across the broken diameter and very heavy. She wished she had something to put over it. A newspaper perhaps? She could see no means of obtaining one. She suddenly remembered her cardigan which she had dropped on the grass when she "tackled" her athlete.

For a second she came to a full stop. The cardigan! What a fool she was. She had got half way out of the Square and to turn back now would give anyone a chance of catching up. She cursed her forgetfulness. The excitement of the Plate had put unnecessary extras like cardigans-on-hot-days out of mind.

Then she remembered its usefulness in Gwynod and decided to go back for it. Besides, it shouldn't be left to tell the tale of her visit there. Though what would people think if they saw her with a great wedge of stone under her arm. . . .

But it wasn't stone. Jessica stared down at it. She hadn't given herself time to observe it closely but whereas the disc had certainly looked as stony as everything else about the statue, the Plate had the feel of metal, a dull greenness clouding its surface. As for a pattern on the metal, Jessica could make out nothing.

154

She drew breath and made for the museum path. Some sightseers were meandering towards the entrance and most likely would idle by the statue on the way. She tried to pass them quickly, shuffling her feet behind. They parted and she dashed through, snatched her cardigan from the grass, and ran.

Once she got out of the twist of streets, it was straight downhill to the station. This time she had to find her way to ticket offices and platforms. No train to Duffryn until four o'clock, said the man at the ticket desk. Jessica's expectant, hopeful face fell in dismay.

Three hours to wait in Abertowyn — on her own. Never had provincial country life been better brought home to her than at this moment. London swarmed with trains. But here on a Saturday one train into town was followed, at a distance convenient for a day's shopping, by another train home again. No doubt the same people would be catching it to get back for tea.

Jessica could dawdle as she pleased: it made no difference to what she could accomplish. Her most sickening fear was that the desecration of the statue would be discovered before she got out of Abertowyn. They'd search everybody then as they boarded the train. She'd seen things like that at the pictures. All over Europe they said it was happening. And as a foreigner in Wales she might be specially suspect.

She turned and wandered back up the road. Now that time hung heavy she could actually think about it all — go over events — ponder how easy it had been to dislodge the Plate though in every way it looked a natural part of the disc. Jessica thanked her great-aunt for making her think about riveted china. Had the artist known what he was using? Or was there something about the Plate itself that cheated?

Jessica glanced quickly under her cardigan. It seemed, in the shadow, to be developing a kind of lustre, yet so far there was nothing remotely remarkable about

155

its appearance. Only the feeling it gave.

She found she was sensitive to all kinds of things. The traffic jarred where five days ago she had thought she would never settle to the stillness of country existence.

She noticed that many places had closed for lunch. Queues lined the pavements outside cake shops. The rationing had made people willing to wait hours for an afternoon opening, and even then they could only buy a small slab. A notice in the window stated the weight of cake to which each customer was restricted. The shop keepers did their best, it said, opening two afternoons a week. There were lots of old people in the queue; many ageing men who perhaps had fought in another war, standing there now with shabby shopping bags.

Jessica felt the endless patience of endlessly waiting folk encompass her. She had to wait herself but it was nothing compared to the day-in, day-out waiting that you went through in a time of war.

Her thoughts returned to the Plate. Somehow it wanted her to hurry. She said to herself: "I know I've got to get back to Duffryn. I know I've got to get into the circle again. But I'm stuck."

She walked on, increasingly hungry. If she could find something to eat it would pass some of the time. There was one tea shop she knew which Miss Jones had taken them to. It had been nice, with starched white cloths on every table. The trouble was it was dinner-time and Jessica wanted her money to stretch. Besides, she wouldn't be happy facing waitresses on her own. So she passed the shop and went on walking.

What should she do? She had no intention of going near the museum again. No doubt Ann would have spent her time in that way but Jessica was determined to bury herself and her crime among the shoppers.

She was going towards the town centre, but first she had to pass the turning off to the museum. Jessica crossed the road before she reached that point, and continued on the

156

other side. There were places along here that didn't interest her much, not being of a domestic or glamourous kind: more bicycles, and some farming materials, and gear for home allotments. Only men seemed to be hanging about.

Jessica pressed on, intent on covering ground. Just a little way ahead, shaded by a shop awning, stood the man who had been on the museum bench. Jessica was sure it was him. He was long and thin and slouched in an old mac and a cap even though the day was fine. She remembered how he had turned towards her as she stepped away from the statue. She knew he was staring at her now. And she was such an obvious landmark on this side of the road.

Jessica clutched hard at the Plate. She didn't want to pass the man or go anywhere near him – not even in bright sunlight with people around. She turned to look at the nearest shop, her steps fumbling for direction. She was dimly aware that it was some kind of second-hand furniture place, with one or two items stacked outside on the pavement.

Assuming an improbable interest she bent to examine a table with glinting gluey varnish. All the time her thoughts were on the man. Was he still there? Was he looking in her direction? The cardigan slid away from her arm and she had a sudden glimpse of the Plate. It had lessened considerably in weight and exactly matched in appearance the yellow oak she was bending over.

Jessica started up to face the street. The man had gone from where she had last seen him. She walked forward in a kind of stupor, aware only that the Plate was gaining in weight and becoming metal between her fingers.

Ahead of her was traffic and shops more to her liking if only she could have concentrated on them. Ideas about the Plate spilled through her head. It had definitely been stone when she found it. Even though she'd accepted afterwards that it was an old mouldy bit of metal. But Duguth had talked about it as a treasure of the Cenarti, a work of superlative imagination, with its own peculiar power.

157

She joined the people on the kerb waiting for the policeman to wave them across the street. It was hot, it was Saturday, and her feet were aching. She wanted to find a milk bar but the crowd was too solid to see through.

As if she had received a slap Jessica rocked. The man — the same man — was closer than he had ever been. He was crossing beside her. He was keeping in exact step with her.

Jessica stopped dead on the other side to examine her sandal. Be careful, Duguth had said. Be very careful once you find the Plate of Alquar.

When she looked up the man had gone — Jessica wished she knew in which direction. She idled a moment or two, then walked on a few yards. A largish store, mainly china and bric-a-brac, stretched for a couple of windows. She could pass five minutes browsing in there to give the man a good start.

She went in with less timidity because it was obviously the place where several people were just looking round. There were decks of dinner service, gilt-edged and impressive; fluted china cups that Jessica thought must be very difficult to drink out of; china dogs and figurines whose prettiness appealed to her; boxes with thick white crockery relegated to floor level as being cheaper stuff for those who would stoop to it. The time passed absorbingly enough and Jessica had only covered a quarter of what the place offered.

A quaintly patterned tea service near the window made her lean forward. People were glancing in all the time but just at this moment Jessica's attention was drawn by one observer. At a bus stop on the kerb slouched a tall mackintoshed man, his face lifted in the direction of the store.

At the same instant as she saw him Jessica became aware of the Plate in her hand taking on a terrible fine smoothness. Her mind could hardly register it before her fingers felt it slipping. As she gaped at the man the Plate of Alquar, now a fragile piece of china, fell from her grasp.

158

17

As Ann drew the wave over them there came a rushing, hissing darkness. How long it lasted she did not know, but she felt she had gone very deep down under the earth or beneath the sea, and that she was standing in a tunnel like the first passage into Caer Owen.

Instinctively and very slowly she walked forward into the darkness. It seemed to her, strangely enough, that there was nothing to be afraid of. Glyn Evans' account of coal mines came into her head. There was danger — always. But miners lived with darkness all the time. Pit ponies had had to live with darkness. And people too, every day or night of their lives when they fell asleep went into a kind of darkness. Even the blackout had simply re-taught every-body a natural communion with the night.

Ann went on, aware that she was coming to a deep and slow-moving river. Nothing gave out light, yet she knew that there was a long, slender craft with bare-breasted oars-men waiting. In the rear of the boat stood the motionless figure of a man, shaded by greater darkness.

Ann was beckoned to step into the boat and sit behind the tall dark figure. Then the men raised their shelved oars and with one push the boat went out into mid-stream.

She knew they were gliding fast, though the waters did not ripple. A stronger current beneath the surface was taking them with it.

She glanced up at the man standing a few feet in front. He seemed to merge more completely than anyone into the dark that held them. The oars she could see clearly dipping on either side, the bare arms of the men elbowed back with a steady rhythm. But this man she was close to was all shadow to her.

159

The darkness grew, if possible, more intense, until the boat and its crew and the motionless man were one indistinguishable presence and Ann felt her own identity fade until she flowed like the river. Little by little awareness of change stole over her. The thought of light came into her head and almost imperceptibly light grew, with the slowness of a plant growing or a flower opening.

Ann could see now that the man was bronze and his flesh shone as if oil had anointed it. When she looked up at his head a sliver of light shone so brightly above it that it could hardly be gazed at. It grew and rounded into a huge disc whose brightness covered all the man's shoulders. Ann could no longer see those who travelled in the front of the boat for the light had risen between.

She became aware of people on the bank; thousands crowding to welcome them, as if warmth and life proceeded from the boat. Ann recalled, from the stories she knew of Ancient Egypt, how the sun-god Horus sank each night in the west and was rowed through the darkness of the underworld to rise again each morning in the east. So light and dark were united in creation.

Ann closed her eyes for the brightness was blotting out even the sight of the crowded banks, serving as much as the darkness had done to hide things from view. Then she felt a cold wind against her cheek and a lessening of the light on her eyeballs and she found she was blinking at a grey sea with two promontories of land lying far apart and the bay open in its old curve.

Ann gripped the thick roughness of the stone wall to steady herself and turned back into the room where she had left the old man lethargic in his chair. There were doors standing open and Cenarti moving about as if they were emerging from some dream. The old man was on his feet, clutching pathetically at his beard.

"It is long since we have known these things," he cried. "What do you want with us, strange child, bringing such memories?"

160

"I don't know," faltered Ann, "what you have seen."

"We Cenarti," went on the old man passionately, "have been great — in art, in invention, in discovery, in the practice of ancient craft; we have sailed, and fought, and worshipped in the holiest sanctuaries; rough stone has yielded to us the most precious of metals. You do not need to tell me that our existence is half of what it was; that we have grown old and caged and manipulated."

He gazed angrily round, and the younger Cenarti fell back from him. A man entered whose robe was a summer garden of ancient signs, and whose head was the most dome-shaped of all Ann had yet seen.

"We have come," he said in unexcited tones, "because the Ancient One drew us. But we have left our work to do so, and should we be a millimetre out in our calculation of — "

"Go," said the old man, rearing very tall. "Do not be a millimetre out in your calculation!"

He spread-eagled his hands and they all went except Ann. The old man drooped willow-like into his chair.

"What was it you came for?" he asked as if forgetful of everything she had told them.

Ann stood beside him and once again related the need of the Glyphs: their attempt to restore the Plate of Alquar; how they lived a half-existence, labouring hard and fearful of things they could not understand.

Then Ann breathed in the old man's ear the new distress the Glyphs had about their children. She wondered if he actually heard her words, so little sign did he give. At last she told him:

"The young Glyphs would be freed from their darkness if they were united with the young Cenarti."

"Where are the young Cenarti?" asked the old man, turning his burning eyes on her.

Ann was silent. She had seen the young Cenarti and what little youth they had in them.

"It is too late," went on the old man. "We had a vision once, when — "

He glanced slyly towards the wall where part of the Plate of Alquar still gleamed faintly.

"You see," he said. "The Glyphs talk. But they have not restored the Plate which they destroyed. In the same way the bond remains broken between us. They cannot give us the energy to move and we have none of our own to stretch out to them."

"Will it always be like this?" cried Ann. "Always and always?"

"No," said the Ancient One. "There is an end coming. I feel it here, though it is long since I acknowledged that such a spot could teach me anything." He pressed the robe close over his heart.

"I had skills once," he said with puzzled, tired eyes, "that Magob has sought from me, drained from me, during my life. Though not all — the Cenarti do not give up all their secrets or he could dispense with us totally."

"Why do you say the end is coming?" persisted Ann.

"It is something I can tell. Many old instincts are lost to us, that perhaps the Glyphs still retain. But we have the ability to read signs. There is disaster here, built up over Caer Owen. I have sought to know more but it is closed to me. I see only the spiralling hawk ready to descend."

"You have such magnificent things around you," whispered Ann. "Do they not make you want to fight back?"

The old man closed his eyes and shook his head mournfully to and fro against the great carved chair back. Ann went and sat at his feet.

Duguth released Peter gently from his cranny in the rock. He had waded out to Gullzin when the tide sank, aware that the boy had by no means perished but was gazing alertly ahead as if his mind could never leave the mound of Caer Owen. His limbs, however, were numb, unrecognised parts of him, and the cloak he had sought to guard as a precious object was imbued with brine and green weed.

"It's all right," said Duguth. "You can see the fortress now. The sea has restored it to its old position."

Peter looked weakly back at him.

"It was. . .a miracle. . ." he whispered. "I could breathe . . .straight through to. . ."

He coughed and found that once he had begun it was difficult to stop.

"You called on the Power of Air," said Duguth. "I know. But the protection's gone. You're as open to cold as the rest of us so the sooner I get you back to Pengaron the better. Don't talk any more; just rest on me."

The boy was unable to stand. Duguth put his own cloak round him and carried him across to the shore, then on to the road, and so home to Pengaron. Before long Peter was sitting up in warm blankets with Annis tending him and Keith and Marran piling up logs so that the fire might never sink.

"Rest and sleep," ordered Duguth as if he could exert his authority even over natural functions.

The man returned then to the shore and took up his position facing Caer Owen. The Venerables were back on Gullzin and reported no sign of change. Duguth wondered, bitterly, what it was he expected. Jessica had not returned. There was no Plate of Alquar. Why therefore should anything mark out today as different from yesterday?

There was just one possibility, but not even that was taking place. Duguth wondered, now that the fortress was restored, why Magob had not begun once again to close his gates.

"He's waiting for something," he said, feeling the terrible implication of his own thought, "and when it comes it will bring us no joy."

18

"Oh," gasped Jessica.

"Slippery you see, it is, this fine china," said a woman's voice. "Here you are, my dear. Hold it tight."

It was the same woman who had spoken to Jessica before about the weather. Small, bow-legged. She'd seen her on some street, outside some shop. And now this little woman, pert as a robin, had caught in both hands the Plate of Alquar.

"Oh," gasped Jessica again, and this time it was a wail of relief.

"Pretty, isn't it?" said the woman, lingering with it in her grasp. "But broken already I see."

"Yes," said Jessica. "I'm having it replaced."

It was awkward the way it looked like the set they were standing near. As if she'd picked it up off the counter.

"I would look after it," said the woman, "if I were you."

Jessica thanked her and straightaway left the shop. The Plate grew in weight and thickness as she went through the door.

The man had gone from his post though Jessica hadn't noticed any bus going by. It was silly of her to bother about him. Silly to have this hunted feeling. All the same she wanted to get away from these streets. She didn't trust any of the people around, jostling and startling her, making her lose her grip. On a Saturday afternoon all the villagers in Wales must have poured into town.

She caught sight of a milk bar on the other side of the road. She could afford that and it would be a relief to sit down. When she got across she found the place warm and cramped. She wondered how, with an arm clamped tightly round the Plate she was going to carry more than one article

164

from the counter. Under ordinary circumstances she might have put her belongings down to reserve a seat; but not the Plate of Alquar.

She decided to forego having a drink for a while and chose a sticky bun. Then she took the third place at a table for four. It was in fact only big enough for two but Jessica was thin and squeezed sideways into the narrow corner. She could see at the next table along a man whose capacious frame so overhung the spindly seat that he might have been sitting on air.

She thought it best to ignore the couple into whose company she had intruded and applied herself, eyes down, to her bun. She was aware that the young man and woman next to her were saying a great deal more to each other with their eyes and their cigarette smoke than with their voices. Jessica disliked smoke and didn't know why the girl's cherried mouth sucking at the cigarette stub should appear in any way attractive to the young man. The girl in any case looked scornfully in Jessica's direction as if she were thinking: little pitchers have big ears.

"I can't help it," thought Jessica. "There's nowhere else to sit."

She had the boldness now to glance round. The walls were decorated with photos of current film heart throbs, the men with sleek hair, the women with waves short and waves long and all of them with thickly crimsoned mouths and large dewy eyes. Jessica spent a few minutes spotting them, while the couple beside her went on with their wordless converse.

The trouble with an iced bun, Jessica decided, was that you couldn't sit over it for ever. Not like the stone cold tea her companions were taking hours to finish. She contemplated getting up and collecting a lemonade. It meant disturbing the young man next to her in the middle of blowing rings of smoke. Then if she had to come back. . .

She looked round quickly for the possibility of another seat. At a table on the other side of the passageway sat a

165

mackintoshed figure. Jessica didn't wait long enough to discover if it were the man from the museum bench. She was up in a flash, almost angry, had pushed past the startled youth quite rudely and made for the door.

Only just in time she shied away from a replica of the J. Arthur Rank gong, clutching hard at the Plate, willing it not to change into *that*. Then she was out of the shop and round the corner before, she hoped, the man could get to the door.

She was going in the right direction for the station though it wasn't the main road she was on. She had time to twist round corners, to place street blocks between herself and whatever pursued.

The Plate was an uncomfortable hot weight; the muscles in her elbow ached with the strain of cradling it.

All around her now was a web of terraced stone cottages opening onto narrow pavements. Every now and then she caught a sight of hill beyond, with bushy green patches. She had lost the town centre; had she also come too far down for the station, she wondered?

There were children playing out in the road, so she could always ask her way. Jessica slowed down, panting. She guessed she was coming to a factory area from the character of the buildings, and her spirits sank.

She turned and looked back up the street, debating what to do. It struck her that everything was clean and scrubbed about the place, and there was a woman even on Saturday afternoon rubbing her doorstep. Hard work and a strict life and pride in it too came through to Jessica, from the spruce nets at the narrow windows to the carefully painted drainpipes. With the Plate glowing against her stomach she was seeing things she had never taken account of before.

As she stood at the foot of the street, a man came into view at the other end. He was tall, mackintoshed, slouching; he stopped and simply stared towards her.

Jessica's heart pounded, but she remained where she was.

166

The man also didn't move. It struck her that continuous as his presence might be, he was set only on observing. The thought crossed her mind: he's just the first stage.

Chilled right through in spite of the sun, but with dignity now, Jessica turned a corner, asked someone to direct her to the station, and walked slowly on.

The station was noisy and hazed with steam. The Porthglas train, she was told, was due out at ten past three.

Oh, thought Jessica, but the man said —

He must have made a mistake and missed out on the three-ten — perhaps it ran only on Saturdays. She knew the Porthglas train ran through Duffryn. It was the one Miss Jones had taken them on. Her train earlier that day had come from Porthglas. Jessica felt it was a stroke of luck. In five minutes she would be out of Abertowyn.

Once in the coach she strained against the window to see if her pursuer was still following. The platform was too crowded for her to be sure, but she saw no one like him come through the barrier.

Jessica settled with relief to watching the hillsides as the train wound up through the valley. It was fast now, racing as she wanted it to. The Plate rested heavily in her lap, still concealed by her cardigan. She let her eyes close against the sun's brightness. At this time on a hot day everybody and everything seemed jaded. The sun had a denser, more throbbing force. The wheels too were throbbing in her head. Soon, and soon, and soon, they said. It will all be over soon.

They were going at a tremendous pace, steam flying. Jessica watched it drift in long swathe shadows across the landscape.

More rattling erupted into the compartment as the ticket inspector slid open the door. This time Jessica had her ticket ready, but he shook his head over it.

"Why not?" she asked, feeling her voice click in her throat. She had an instinctive knowledge of what was coming.

167

"Because we are going all the way through to Porthglas," said the man. "It would be the four o'clock you want. That is a stopping train now."

"What do I do?" mouthed Jessica.

"Don't go white, girl," said the man. "I won't charge you more. It is a genuine mistake I am sure. Only you will have to wait at Porthglas for a train back to Duffryn, and that might be a little while into the evening. You could see the station master about it and he might say that you needn't pay again in the circumstances."

The man was nice. So nice that Jessica nearly cried. What she wanted had nothing to do with paying for tickets.

He left her cursing her own folly. "Damn," she said inwardly, having acquired something from Peter.

Now she understood how she had been pushed into getting back to the station just in time to rush onto this miserable train and not early enough to discover the truth about it. She'd felt even before finding the Plate the danger of being forced into things. Yet she'd let it happen. How else was it that she was exactly where she shouldn't be, off course, with no means of remedying the situation? It was worse when she came to think of it than being stuck in Abertowyn.

The train shot through Duffryn. She watched the last familiar landmarks disappear from view. She glimpsed the road that went round the hill and west to Pengaron. Further back from the station you would come to the bramble hedge. . . .

Nothing ahead of Jessica was familiar. The country loomed, repeating hillsides and farms and trees, but Jessica knew, with a sickening deadness inside her that it was as strange and undistinctive to her as the ice floes of the Arctic would have been.

Peter slept, but awoke fitfully, half aware, half submerged. He knew he was alone in the room, except perhaps for the baby in her cot. Annis he could hear out in the yard and no doubt Keith and Marran had been given this last hour off before the evening closed in and Magob drew them into his tighter circle.

Peter lay peacefully for a while, trying to think. Something about Magob stirred his memory. His whole body was aching, but there was something else, something that was making his arm itch.

He shot bolt upright. It was the letters forged into his shoulder. He must call An–

No! He mustn't call anyone. Not by name. That was something he understood dimly, for he remembered that it was speaking his own name that had done so much damage.

He must get out of here. If Magob could observe through him he must release this place of his presence. He was a walking danger.

He shook free of the blankets and pulled on clothes. The cloak was drying in front of the fire but it was still fairly sodden, so Peter abandoned it. He was halfway to the door when Duguth entered.

"Dug–" Peter began but did not finish. Instead he said as if he were going to be sick: "Got to get out. Don't stop – "

"What is it?" asked Duguth forcefully, for Peter's eyes were bulging.

The boy clasped his arm for answer, and Duguth drew Peter with him through the yard and out up the lane. When they had rounded the corner from the village, Duguth stopped.

"Now tell me," he said.

"It's beginning to burn," said Peter. "You said that Magob could spy on the village through me. I've got to get away."

"I can't allow it," said Duguth. "It's getting on for dusk and for your own sake you mustn't be out of the village."

"I was last evening," said Peter.

"He had a job then for you. If you leave us now he could destroy you."

"But — the others?"

"You won't be able to hurt them," said Duguth softly, "because you don't want to. Don't struggle with it any more Peter. I will face what comes."

The boy groaned and relaxed all of a sudden.

"Peter," something inside his head called relentlessly. "Peter. Peter." He was reminded of the nagging enquiry he had experienced in the cellar of Caer Owen. He kept his eyes fixed on Duguth. The man looked straight back at him.

Suddenly Peter exclaimed: "Duguth!" Then again: "Duguth. Duguth."

They both waited.

"I — can't — remember — " said Peter as if answering someone. "If I see them — "

He turned back in the direction of the village, but Duguth swung him round.

The man knew he had to appear a rough farmer. Magob was looking through Peter now and it was important that he saw nothing of the truth.

"What don't you remember, boy?" he asked, as if irritated after a day's labour in the fields.

"The names," said Peter. "The names of the others. If I see them, though, I'll remember."

He tried again to turn back into the village but Duguth held onto him.

"Foolish boy," said Duguth, "always forgetting things."

"I — must — see — them. I will know them."

"Oh no you don't," said Duguth. "You're the most useless one among us, eating us out of house and home. Today you can stand out in the cold. I won't allow you from this spot."

The boy fought him then, but the tussle could have only one end. Peter was strong, but not as strong as the man.

"Duguth, Duguth, Duguth," shouted Peter. "*His* name's Duguth."

170

The man felt a power encompassing him, nosing like a dog and bringing with it a sickening stench. They were standing close to a yew, the conifer tree of grief, which had grown slowly and persistently over the years in accord with the Glyphs' sadness and now bore a rich crop of flaming berries. Duguth dragged Peter away from its cascading green embrace and out into the open. He felt Magob's power waver a little and thin out.

Peter was sweating under his grip, straining to follow where Magob was luring. Duguth remembered that he had only recently come through another physical ordeal after a night without sleep, and wondered how soon the boy's strength would give way altogether.

He had not long to wait before Peter dropped into incoherence. While Magob looked and listened through him he could only have seen the lane into Pengaron and a Glyph farmer in a vindictive temper. No damage had been done and Duguth guessed that Magob would not reckon Peter among his most valuable of spies.

He picked the boy up once more and carried him back into Annis's house. The inflammation had died down on Peter's shoulder.

"He must sleep," he warned the women. "And you must not let him out of your sight."

Later Duguth stood on the shore gazing at the retreating tide. Two horns of land were beginning once more to close round in an arc. In another hour what was left of the thinning water in the bay would be no more than a lake. It would lie still when the full moon shone on its surface that night because it would be out of the pull of the world's tides.

Here was the greatest of Magob's gates closing, and when it was fully shut then all the other entrances to Gwynod would be barred. Jessica had less than one hour now, by Duguth's reckoning. It would all be over by this day's dusk.

*

Duguth had said something about roads having power to take you home. Jessica could see one now, snaking idly not far from the railway track. Every now and then it disappeared from view beyond fields, but she supposed it must be the road between Duffryn and Porthglas.

She remembered when she and Ann had followed Magob's "wall" round from Duffryn, going north across fields and hedges and streams. Duffryn had lain a good way to the south of the ring so they had gone round behind Pengaron and up in the direction of Porthglas before the curve had taken them towards the sea.

Jessica tried to think where Duguth had said the gates were. She had expected to re-enter the circle by simply stepping off the train and walking out of the station by the wicket. Duffryn was obviously a main gateway to Gwynod. There had been the road over the bridge and the wicket gate and the road that went south which cut between the station and the hedge. As they'd gone further north, however, there was another road that joined Porthglas to Pengaron. But that was when they'd curved well round towards the sea. Duguth had also mentioned the stile as a small entry that might close last. That was why Ann had felt the force drop just there. She herself had flitted for a brief instant out of the circle. . . .

Jessica looked quickly out of the window to see if she had any chance of sighting the place, but decided that they must be well past it by now. It wasn't true, though, that the whole area was strange. She'd been part of the way before on foot and both the railway and the road had run outside the circle. She recalled how the road had lain a bit further up from the stile and had run beside a copse of fir trees, making her think of Christmas. It was the last they'd seen of it before they swung over to the sea.

Jessica was aware suddenly that the train was slowing. They were passing cottages and farmhouses whose rough stone blocks she could trace in detail. Something must be halting them. Sheep on the line? Cattle crossing? The

172

farmers would surely know the times of trains. A hitch, maybe, in getting a herd over, or coal trucks shunted too late across the tracks? The signals had given warning and the train was merely creeping in the hope that it would not have to stop entirely.

Jessica darted up and out of the compartment. Her coach was near the end, so hardly anybody saw a girl lower herself down while the wheels were still doing their slow grind, hardly noticed her hopping gingerly across rails into gorse that came up to her waist. The country was open before her, the air more abundantly free than she had ever felt it before. With her cardigan hugging the burdenous Plate, and the glory of a green world around, Jessica made across the field towards the road on the seaward side of the track, at the same time bearing back the way they had come.

She had a long trek ahead in a vast, solitary world, and she must fly, for the time allowed had almost run out.

Jessica knew she was late. Instinct would have told her had not the sun also declared it. She seemed to have been going for hours until evening clouds mounted over the hill.

She ran with all the swiftness of which she was capable, then rested by reducing her pace to a walk to draw breath. At first she kept to the road, then where possible to the grassy reaches bordering it, looking out all the time for a copse of firs. The valley clove deeper at the Porthglas end than it did at either Duffryn or Abertowyn, the hillside on her left rose steep and on the seaward side the ground undulated endlessly.

The Plate had become a familiar disability by this time: she could feel her heart hammering against it. Jessica would have won any race in her school games with her present speed, for in that alone was her hope.

The place she was making for would be the last gate. If the stile would not let her through then all the other entrances would be closed to her, even supposing she could ever reach them, which she doubted, for there would be no more energy left in her.

She was fighting against something else, too. Not only was she tired and hollow with hunger but the landscape frightened her. Dusk hadn't arrived yet but the thought came: what shall I do when it gets dark? A sizeable bird rising at a distance made Jessica think of eagles. The long grass reminded her of something that Peter had said about Wales being full of adders.

There were fears her mother had drilled into her about the dangers of lonely paths. Suppose someone came by in a car on the empty road and dragged her off? Suppose there were robbers or murderers lurking in bushes or ditches, over the next incline, beyond the next hedge? Tramps would lie out in country like this. The mackintoshed pursuer came to mind. She was running back into the net now and somewhere he would be waiting.

Take care, Duguth had said. Once you have found the Plate, take great care. But what was she to take care of? Where was Magob now?

Jessica gave a gulp for breath. From the top of a slope she could see something dark — the darkness of a fir plantation. She looked eagerly to see if the road wound near. The road seemed in fact to disappear when it came up to it but no doubt it had simply rounded the trees in a curve. If she reached that point, Jessica decided, she could strike out into the fields for it was just about there that the stile lay.

She danced like quicksilver towards the firs. As she neared them she turned onto the rough grazing land sloping first down on her right with a series of hedges and gates and then up against the sky. Jessica ran until she caught sight of a stile.

Would it be the right one? Her leg scraped against something hard, jolting her into stopping. When she reached out her fingers touched sparkling crystal. Jessica gave a sharp cry. The wall, of course. The wall of Gwynod, there

174

in its brilliancy, like diamond-charged rain.

Just as surely as she knew this was the place, she knew also she was being followed. There were sounds behind her but she shut her ears to them. She must get through now, if she had the chance.

She reached the stile and passed her hand across it before mounting. There was a gap — she could feel the edges of crystal, invisible except where the tips of her fingers pressed it into view. The space was narrower than last time but she was slender enough to pass through.

Her foot was on the first step when she heard a voice. What Jessica had not been expecting was a woman's voice. Calling her name! She half turned, twisting against the hand gripping the stile.

Then "Jessica. Darling," came faintly with the wind. The girl stopped altogether. She could have sworn it was her mother's voice. Surely not here, not out in a field between Duffryn and Porthglas. She swung round from the first step and looked.

There *was* a woman coming towards her from the road. And it *was* her mother.

"Jessica. We're here. Wait for me."

Her mother would be slow, naturally, coming through long grass and furze. She'd tear her stockings if she wasn't careful. The figure swayed towards her, making little detours round cow patts.

"Jessica. Why don't you come here? It's Mummy."

Jessica turned back to the stile. She felt with her one free hand for the barrier and found crystal where before there had been air. The gap was closing. Oh, she gasped, struggling to get up another step. Three only and then over. Could she squeeze through? It came to her suddenly that once over she'd be *there*, in Gwynod, and lost to her mother as her mother would be lost to her. It was a thought she couldn't bear.

Oh, she gasped again in agony and thought of telling her mother all about it. Mummy would understand.

The tears were streaming down Jessica's cheeks. Ann and Peter seemed such a long way off. Jessica's immediate need was the important thing. She put up a hand, hoping it would decide for her. The gap, she thought, wouldn't take her now. No good trying. The walls were too close.

She dropped off the stile and ran to meet her mother. For a moment something flashed with crystalline brilliancy as the gates of Gwynod came together. Jessica clung sobbing to her mother, unable to escape the full knowledge that now it was too late. The quest could no longer be fulfilled.

Duguth watched the last inches of land come together before he turned back to Pengaron. The declining day matched Magob's imprisoning power, laying its own melancholy gloom on the world. The sea sounded from a distance, like the caller at the gates it had become.

The man went, eclipsed, to Annis's house. Peter still slept. Duguth gazed slowly round — at Keith and Marran, beginning to move heavily towards the coming night; at Annis and his aunt with their enduring patience; at the homely comfort of plates and table and fire. His people led a simple life, one that did not fit them to cope with the mysteries Magob tyrannously wielded through the superior skills of the Cenarti.

It must end, however. Not this evening nor any other would Keith and Marran be drawn into Magob's keeping. Not whilst he had the Power of Fire at his disposal.

His aunt came close and said: "The girl has not returned?"

Duguth shook his head.

"It is over now," he said calmly.

He stood gazing down at Peter for some time while Annis prepared food. Then he called his cousin and aunt to him.

"You who are closest to me must understand what it is I have to do. We have gambled and lost. Magob knows of

176

our intended revolt and will not let it go unpunished. We have, besides, something to repay our helpers."

He glanced at Peter who stirred but did not open his eyes.

"I called these children," went on Duguth, "not only because the barrier between our two worlds was egg-shell thin at that moment in time but also because they fulfilled the Order of Alquar as depicted on the Plate. They appeared like a miracle in a place cursed through its children. They were whole, healthy, happy. They had the eagerness that was right for the task ahead. They afforded us hope.

"What has happened to Jessica I have no means of telling, but the two remaining in our world have performed their task well, and we are in their debt. They will be released from Gwynod through the Power of Fire."

The two women were silent, Annis with downcast eyes. Eventually, however, it was she who spoke.

"I think, in their world, there will be scathing too. But they have a right to live through their own troubles, and not die with us."

A movement from the bed made Duguth say:

"Peter, if you want to listen, then sit up and let us have the benefit of your company."

Peter struggled in his blankets to raise himself and look across at the three serious faces. It seemed to him that Annis was sadder than ever. For some time Duguth's voice had penetrated his sleep. There had been mention of releasing them from Gwynod — but something else that he could not understand.

"What did you mean about not dying with you?"

Duguth came and sat beside him while the women went silently back to their preparation.

"Peter," he said, "Jessica has not returned."

"Yes," said Peter, "I followed that."

"And the gates are closed."

"*Are* they? Then what will you do?"

"As the fourth member of the Mandala," said Duguth, "I still have an element at my command. The Power of Fire is the most dangerous of all though on occasion the Power of Water may equal it. Had Jessica returned with the mission fulfilled we would have used it as a weapon against Magob. Now it is useless in that direction.

"The Glyphs have known from the start what I offered them by my plan. They knew too the price of failure. They despaired when their children were threatened. So they listened and let me have my way because of the tenuous link they had through me with the Cenarti.

"Now that the plan has failed they know they are a people walking with death. They would prefer it to a lingering torment at the hands of Magob. The Fire will purge this village before Magob draws one child from us this evening."

"But where will you go?" asked Peter only half understanding.

"We shall stay of course, and the end will be sudden, for the Fire will be no ordinary one. As soon as every man is home from his work this day, we shall join to create our own circle and the flame that will rise will glow more welcome than any beacon in a dangerous sea.

"Do not fear, Peter. At the first kindling the Fire Power will release you to the place where you belong. No, do not speak. There are shadows deepening in your world also, or it would never have been our fate to meet in the first place."

19

Jessica wept on her mother's shoulder. It passed like a shower as she listened to the other's story, not able as yet to tell her own.

"Wanted to see you darling. And to know you're well. Peter's parents are coming this weekend."

"And Ann's mother?"

"No — she couldn't you know. At any rate we reached this place called Aber — "

"Abertowyn."

"If you tell me it is. Then imagine, we had to get another train because you're so far out. And what they put us on was all wrong. Get out they said at Duffryn, but we never stopped there and had to go all the way through to — "

"Porthglas!"

Oh, what a fool she'd been. Her mother had been on the same train as herself. The three-ten from Abertowyn. They would have been waiting together on the platform. Jessica laughed a little hysterically.

"Well darling, we took a taxi from there. And what a job we had finding one. You'd think there was only one in the whole country. I saw you from the road you know. I could hardly believe it but — "

"Is Daddy with you?"

"Of course. He just had to come because you know how I need to have things carried. I don't know how I would have managed on my own, with all those names to remember."

Jessica squeezed her arm. She had begun to feel much more independent than her mother.

"These fields are dreadful for one's shoes," said the woman.

They were tottering very slowly back to the road.

"Where is — ?"

"Further up somewhere," said her mother. "Daddy didn't get out of the taxi in case the driver made off with our things."

"Oh but they wouldn't," said Jessica quickly. "Not in these parts."

"Well, we weren't sure you know. Then I wanted so much to be the first to surprise you."

She had made no enquiry as yet about what her daughter was doing out alone in the countryside.

A slope presented itself between them and the road.

"Look," said Jessica, "it'll be easier further on."

"Just as you say. But darling, what are you carrying? Let me see. Oh, do throw it away. It's an old dirty bit of metal."

Jessica had decided to put on her cardigan, cool now after her long run. She glanced down at the Plate whose rim had niched itself into a red groove in her hand. Her mother was right about its appearance. It looked dirty, shabby, and contemptible.

Was this the Plate of Alquar? If the Cenarti did still exist they must be as dull and mouldy and useless by now. Had she really come all the way just for this?

The Plate of Alquar had been Peter's quest. She should never have been sent after it. Yet it had come straight out of that statue's hand as if she were the one it was intended for.

As she looked at it again in the advancing half-light it seemed plainer and more featureless than before, though there had never been any figures that she could make out. It had been thrown out of Gwynod all those years ago. Might she not just as well throw it away again? Of what use could it possibly be?

"Throw it away, darling, do."

Yet Jessica for all the prompting could not deal as summarily with the Plate as she had with the stile. They had gone through certain things together and there was a mark imprinted on her hand where she had carried it for so long.

"It's nothing," said Jessica, "really. It's broken you see."

With the words memories rushed back. The Glyphs and Cenarti forever divided. Ann and Peter trapped.

She sought in her pocket for a handkerchief to put between her dinted palm and the metal's edge. There was something there which she had forgotten. Ann's last gift before they entered the tunnel at Caer Owen. *Special*, Ann had said. And she'd given it to her, Jessica, who'd run away once and run away again.

What had the gypsy said all those months ago? Something about holding to the link of three — that one might break it and bring danger — Jessica remembered the silver piece glinting on Ann's palm. She herself was the one who had broken the link, and the others would be waiting for Jessica who never came. These were things she could never tell to her mother.

They arrived at a small stream, trickling low in its bed, and turned up directly towards the road in order to avoid it.

"Really," said her mother, "I didn't think I'd come so far. We haven't missed the road, have we?"

"No," said Jessica. "It's just taken a bend, that's all. And the ground is easier for you here."

"Well, let's stay away from the water." said her mother. "I don't want to get wet as well."

It was too late, in any case, thought Jessica. She couldn't get back into Gwynod now that the gates had closed. She needed no power of imagination to understand that all the other entrances would be sealed against her. Duguth had said she was the only one left who could perform this task of finding the Plate and bringing it back. Oh, she did wish that Duguth wouldn't keep talking to her so. What was it he'd said? Be careful once you have found the Plate, be very careful. Well, she was all right now, wasn't she?

Had Magob won then? She supposed dully that he had.

He hadn't really offered much danger. The mackintoshed man was nothing more than a threat, pushing her into doing silly things, but he hadn't caught up with her or been waiting when she got to the stile. She'd abandoned that last chance of entering Gwynod of her own free will. The chance that had brought her mother to the spot at that very moment in time had offered the greatest temptation of all.

"Do stay away from that water," said her mother suddenly and, to Jessica's surprise, quite irritably.

It was only a small stream. After what she had been through that day the girl would have welcomed the opportunity of taking off her sandals and refreshing her feet. She'd done it before, a few days ago, with Ann.

It flashed through her — there'd been a gap there too, before they reached the stile. Ann had stood mid-stream, sketching at the air. Jessica was surprised Duguth hadn't mentioned that gate, though in any case it would be closed now.

But perhaps it wasn't a gate. Jessica racked hard at her memory. Ann had said something about an old belief. . . running water could cut through fields of force. . .magic couldn't reach you in a stream. . .because the water was running. . .running.

Duguth had said it was all right "while the sea ran into the bay". Not while the sea was in the bay, but while it *ran* into the bay. Oh what was so important about running water?

Jessica stared hard at it. Magob's wall had never been an ordinary one — it had the strength and seeming invincibility of all the natural and magnetic energies he had learnt to draw on. But water had its own natural force. While the stream flowed, Magob's wall could not cross it.

"Jessica, do let's hurry now."

She was aware that her mother had gone several paces ahead, but she didn't run to catch her up. Instead she slipped off her sandals, picked them up in her free hand,

and felt the water trickle over her feet.

Oh Mummy, she thought, I want to tell you, but there isn't time. There's something I've got to find out. It's a second chance, you see.

Her mother's voice called from a distance, but Jessica was sprinting as well as she could through the darkening water. It was flowing softly and while it did she would go with it. Last time she had failed but this time she would shut her ears to all distraction.

But it hurt. She could hardly see for the tears that were streaming down her cheeks. She must call and say it was all right and not to worry if she was late getting back. . . .

Jessica turned and saw a terrible sight. Her mother's form was swaying beside the stream, but at the same time it was vanishing like smoke. The woman seemed so unsubstantial that you would not have called her anything more than a shadow.

Jessica shook. It had never been her mother who met her at the stile. Every bit of it was a cheat. Magob's greatest ally had been herself. Her own weakness had drawn her away from completing the quest.

She turned and splashed along the rill. The fear now was not just of being late, but of being too late. The faces of Annis and her mother rose strong in front of her — serious, sorrowful, with a terrible speechlessness about them.

She must get through this time; that was what mattered. Then the Plate must reach Duguth, which meant a journey ahead of her yet. Jessica had got her wind back since the stile, but she had been shaken in other ways. Her feet squelched over stones embedded in soft clotted soil. The water bed was narrowing, but the ground still took it gently downhill. Suddenly her hand grazed against a hardness in the air that she knew from a quick flash was crystal. The water parted the field of force that was Magob's wall, and Jessica went with it.

It was a colder sky she was under now, the last rays of light streaked pale and high. It must be earlier in the day in Gwynod, but it was the time of year when evening set in equally early. All around, the trees showed clearly their knots of rook nests in barren branches.

Jessica knew she would have to leave the stream (which was splashing icy round her ankles) and cut across country behind Caer Owen, in order to reach Pengaron. She was incredibly weary, her legs ached and everything in her drooped with lack of food. She folded the Plate like a shield across her stomach, and went on.

"Must keep on. . .must keep on. . .rum tum tum. . . rum tum tum. . .must keep on. . . ." sang Jessica's mind, concentrating on any ridiculous set of words it could, while she jog-trotted along. Anything to keep from wondering how Magob would strike next.

She was in Magob's country. She had the Plate. She had come through the barrier. Now she sensed something around her ready to pounce.

Magob would not let her. . .not let. . .get to Pengaron. "Rum tum tum," sang Jessica, "that's my hum. . .here I come. . ."

OH!

It was more than a shriek. Her whole body was thrown onto rough ground. Stones slid. Pain splashed, scalding, through her and was released in bitter tears.

For a long time she lay sprawled in misery. Then as the pain drew back into a spot that could be located, she made an effort to sit up. The twist in her foot wouldn't allow her even to do so much. Desperately, angrily, Jessica knew that she was out of the race.

Somewhere the Plate had fallen too. She managed to raise herself onto bruised elbows and peered around. Nothing but large slabs of stone met her gaze. She knew she had to look for a certain shape. Perhaps that was it, a few yards ahead. Between twinges she dragged herself across to the flat whitish object.

She needed to know, and she could only find out if it transformed itself back again. She rested on one elbow and lifted the Plate shakily away from its companion stones. Are you the Plate of Alquar? she asked, gripping the rim with the same tenacity as she was clenching her teeth. Then she raised it as high in the air as she could. Staring up at the broken edge outlined against the sky she felt with astonishment the great weight gradually become much lighter.

Ann sat on the tesselated floor, her head resting against the old man's knee. More Cenarti had come to join them and through the doorway she could see others drifting aimlessly down corridors and waiting in further rooms, as if aware of some difference about to affect their torpid lives.

Only the old man and Ann herself were absolutely still. The girl was surprised at how close she felt to the Ancient One. Among the Glyphs she had felt at home. Their way of life was a very recognisable one, having been at a standstill for many generations. But the Cenarti had outstripped the Glyphs in point of time and belonged in some distant future that Ann felt a stranger to. Yet in spite of her awe Ann had crept up to the Ancient One's feet and settled there as her sympathy went out to his defeated pride and helpless sorrow.

She understood now what the Mandala meant — the square fixed within the circle. Neither of these two peoples could flourish cut off from the other. The Glyphs needed inspiration from the Cenarti, and the Cenarti must acknowledge the energies of the Glyphs. There was a kind of balance demanded by the universe which the Cenarti, for all their proud learning, could not defy.

The old man's chair faced down the room towards the window where the light struggled to enter. He did not move his head, but his eyes could travel, glittering, across to the small patch of wall between curtains and tapestry. At the moment all shadow seemed to draw into it.

"What is that noise?" asked the old man suddenly.

"Gulls, I think," said Ann, lifting her head to listen.

185

It was a familiar sound to her since she had come to Pengaron.

"I have not listened to them for many years," said the old one. "They sound free."

"I think they're wonderful," said Ann, trying to blaze up a new interest in him. "They look so clean. Their white feathers are such a pure white — "

The time passed in a hushed, refined kind of way. The Cenarti stood with their fading glories around them, as their tide went out. Ann wondered if the old man was thinking of the sea and how it had filled the lives of his ancestors. She had seen it depicted over and over again in their art.

But the old man was watching the shadows. The Cenarti had studied the sky long enough to know how important darkness was to a sighting of the stars. Not that it was stars he was looking for this time, but something much closer and more personal. One of the faculties in him above ordinary sight or sound said: "Look!" And the old man did not take his eyes from the patch of wall.

Then out of the shadow the Plate of Alquar began to glint. With neither sunlight nor firelight on it, a glow appeared, like a full moon. Had it come from the window itself it might indeed have been the full moon rising before its time. But it came from the wall where the old man had fixed his gaze, where the broken Plate of Alquar had rested all the years the Cenarti had been locked away in Caer Owen.

Half the disc glowed solid and the other half was no more than an ethereal light, but together they made up the whole. The Ancient One rose with the energy of an electric current darting through him. Ann sprang up too, startled, and looked across to where they were all gazing.

If she had recognised beauty in the Plate when she first saw it, enough to tell her that of all their treasures the Cenarti would count this supreme, it was something far beyond mere craftsmanship that she beheld now. The circle was a full gold orb and its inset square gave off a

186

vivid ray. At each of the corners was a face so clearly depicted that Ann gasped. Tendrilled between was a world of nature that the artist had observed distinctively and lovingly. It *was* magic that the Plate held, but the greatest magic was in its wholeness.

The Ancient One could only totter, but he alone dared to approach the Plate. His thin arms stretched out as if to receive a child, and the Cenarti trembled as he took it between both hands.

The room was densely packed. Mothers had brought young children, solemn-faced, in their arms. It was as if the Cenarti were ready — for what, Ann could not tell — but they all caught their breath as the old man turned and held high over his head the legendary treasure. The light did not waver; the Plate the Ancient One held up to his people's gaze was as complete as it had once been.

The old man's look struck Ann terrifyingly. The masking languor had cracked, was peeling. His gaunt face was terrible with strength long since left in abeyance. How had she ever dared to pity him?

"The Glyphs have restored the Plate of Alquar," he called, "and the bond is remade. Unlock the doors. Now is the time for us to go forth."

Duguth was holding his aunt and Marran by the hand as they joined in the last family circle. Peter dreaded what was to come. He had cast about for some other answer while the light lingered, drawing out these final moments. Nothing but blankness had come as he watched Annis move softly round her home. Finally she had picked up Gwilla in her arms to join the others in the circle.

Duguth would not include Peter.

"Stay," he ordered when Peter wanted to stand with them. "This is not your fate."

"I *will* join you," said Peter frantically.

Annis quietly shook her head, stilling him into helplessness.

187

Duguth did not reply. He was aware that in every home throughout the village, as men returned from their labours, the circle was being formed. The final moment was near, for the light was going. Duguth knew he had only to turn his thoughts to the Power of Fire. One flame in the midst of the circle —

It flashed before him. Duguth dropped his companions' hands and stared. He had *not* called the Power to him. He had *not* lit that one little flame that was needed. Something else was burning there, something round and flaming in space. The Plate of Alquar flashed suddenly in its splendour in the still room and was gone.

Duguth flung open the door and strode into the air. The sound startled others and there was a series of lifting latches. Peter cried: "Take me with you." But Duguth was past hearing.

The road carried him to the coast where Magob's fort was throbbing like a volcano.

Ann slid by the wall as the Cenarti began to move, unhurriedly, out of the room, along corridors, through halls, crowding each set of doors until they came to the final barrier. At the far end, beyond a small ante-room, stood the last portal.

The great bolts were drawn back to reveal the central stairs by which the Cenarti had entered the upper territory of Caer Owen. Now the Ancient One led, with the Plate of Alquar, and his people came after.

Ann watched as men, women, and children went by. They were a fantastic sight in their long patterned robes but in addition they were clinging to things that marked their former greatness. Men with pale faces carried swords and shields that had been wrought for nobles of the tribe. Women who were thin-lipped and stony-eyed dragged with them the decorations of beauties of long ago. Down the steps they heaved Cenarti treasures, for what their ancestors had brought into Caer Owen they were taking

188

with them in their exodus.

It was a slow and sometimes ghastly procession that descended toward the castle doors, led by an old man whose body trembled from step to step but whose spirit was a searching fire.

Surely, thought Ann, Magob wouldn't allow them to go. Not like this, taking along their finest possessions. Why couldn't they escape quickly, before he moved against them? If only, she thought, they had the legs of the Glyphs they would not totter with their swords and their paintings and their sculptures.

When the flooding mass reached its halfway mark the Boujacks scampered out to face them. The first ones came with an armoury of grins, though each carried iron in his hand. Forming a cordon across the stairs they sought to persuade their subject people to return.

When the Cenarti continued to descend, however, other Boujacks were quick to appear behind the first, stolid and bright, all with metal clubs. Ann gasped as she slid round a bend in the stairs, for every flight down to the fortress doors was now thronged with the glowing, menacing mass of indistinguishable men and heavy weapons.

How could the Cenarti, weakened by long years within the fort, pass that thick and malevolent barrier? The Boujacks advanced together like a battering ram towards their foremost ranks.

But the Cenarti did not see them. Friendly persuasion and brute force were alike to them, for the Cenarti were leaving Magob's fort and nothing now could stop them. The old man held up the Plate of Alquar and it returned upon the enemy, scintillating, their own vivid callousness. Its field of force cracked open the Boujacks' ranks and the Ancient One passed with not a hand, not a weapon, reaching him. Those coming behind swept on, their old power grown faint but never lost entirely, so that the Boujacks who were prevented from tumbling back were pressed hard to the sides of the stairs.

Waiting on the shore Duguth had the vision of a great sea flowing through the fort, crested by an old man holding aloft a flashing emblem. He raised his own arms in return, like a beacon ready to flame forth.

Back in Pengaron the Glyphs in their homes or their yards, turning out at gates or unsnecking doors, looked up and beheld the Cenarti winding relentlessly down the centre of Caer Owen. Peter in the midst of Annis's family glimpsed only for a second that strange people moving step by step out of their imprisonment.

In the fortress itself Ann was carried forward by the surge. Although she could not walk beside the Ancient One she could still see that resolute face beneath the white hair.

Jessica, lying winded in the field, saw the half-Plate in her hand flame and the light draw into a complete circle. With one elbow propped in the stubbly grass she held the weightless disc high against the sky. Four figures shone from its corners. At the centre was an old man leading his people out of captivity.

There sounded in Pengaron that night, from another fold of time, the cry of a new-born child. Jessica knew, as Ann knew and Peter knew, that their mission was complete.

A rumbling began, faint but increasing, through the stones of Caer Owen.